ROSAMUND

ALSO BY SHANI STRUTHERS

EVE: A PSYCHIC SURVEYS PREQUEL

PSYCHIC SURVEYS BOOK ONE:
THE HAUNTING OF HIGHDOWN HALL

PSYCHIC SURVEYS BOOK TWO:
RISE TO ME

PSYCHIC SURVEYS BOOK THREE:
44 GILMORE STREET

PSYCHIC SURVEYS BOOK FOUR:
OLD CROSS COTTAGE

PSYCHIC SURVEYS BOOK FIVE:
DESCENSION

BLAKEMORT
(A PSYCHIC SURVEYS COMPANION NOVEL BOOK ONE)

THIRTEEN
(A PSYCHIC SURVEYS COMPANION NOVEL BOOK TWO)

THIS HAUNTED WORLD BOOK ONE:
THE VENETIAN

THIS HAUNTED WORLD BOOK TWO:
THE ELEVENTH FLOOR

JESSA*MINE*
(JESSAMINE SERIES BOOK ONE)

COMRAICH
(JESSAMINE SERIES BOOK TWO)

A Psychic Surveys Companion Novel
Book Three

ROSAMUND

SHANI STRUTHERS

Psychic Surveys Companion Novel Book Three, Rosamund
Copyright © Shani Struthers 2019

The right of Shani Struthers to be identified as the Author of the work has been asserted by her in accordance with the Copyright, Designs and Patents Act 1988.

All rights reserved in all media. No part of this publication may be reproduced, stored in a retrieval system, or transmitted in any form or by any means, electronic, mechanical, recording, photocopying, the Internet or otherwise, without the prior written consent of the copyright holder, nor be otherwise circulated in any form of binding or cover other than that in which it is published and without a similar condition being imposed on the subsequent purchaser.

Storyland Press
www.storylandpress.com

ISBN: 978-1-7939-0833-9

All characters and events featured in this publication are purely fictitious and any resemblance to any person, place, organisation/company, living or dead, is entirely coincidental.

As much as I love writing, building a relationship with readers is even more exciting! I occasionally send newsletters with details on new releases, special offers and other bits of news relating to the Psychic Surveys series as well as all my other books. If you'd like to subscribe, sign up here!

www.shanistruthers.com

For Patricia Kearsey, thank you for your support and encouragement throughout my writing career and your kind words when my mum passed – fly free and enjoy your next adventure.

Acknowledgements

Rosamund Davis – Ruby's great grandmother – has intrigued me ever since I started to write the Psychic Surveys series. She has only ever been alluded to throughout but even so, it was clear she was a woman of great substance, not afraid to delve into the world of spirit as well as *non*-spirit, sharing her work with others so that they may learn how to deal with such matter in a safe manner. And so, of course, I had to find out more about this enigmatic woman and thus write a companion novel dedicated to her and her alone. Setting a book in the early twentieth century was a challenge for me, getting the speech right as well as many historical facts. Thank you especially to Robert Struthers for painstakingly helping me with this. It is important to note that, for the sake of a good story, some poetic license has been used with facts here and there, but for the main part everything should ring true. Thank you also to my tireless beta readers, Louisa Taylor, Amelia Haire, Lesley Hughes, Gina Dickerson and Corinna Edwards-Colledge, your input as always is invaluable. Thanks to my editor too, Vee McGivney, and, once again, to Gina Dickerson for formatting and all artwork. Psychic Surveys is the story that just keeps on giving, I never guessed when I started it that I would 'meet' so many fascinating and strong women, and amongst them, Rosamund is one of my favourites. I hope you enjoy reading about her.

Prologue

1889

THIS is why I do it. Why I write.

It is not comfortable where I am sitting. It is a small space, cramped. In front of me is a child's desk, and barely any light to see by, just a pale shaft that shines through a small oval window. How valiant that light is; how it tries so hard to pierce the gloom. My hands, oh my hands! They shake as I scribe, guilty of knocking over the inkpot on several occasions. Not that it matters about the spillage. Not here, in the attic. He will not see it. He refuses to venture in here. As to why, I have no clue. Perhaps he is afraid, although it holds far less to be frightened of than what dwells in his mind. There *are* things to be frightened of, however… strange things…

I do not have long. The day is beginning to wane and soon I will not be able to see to write – not anymore. My hands shaking worse than ever, I add to the quantity of paper already filled. I outline; I describe. Sometimes in fleeting detail, at other times so much more than that, even though my heart threatens to burst from my chest because of it and my head screams: *'Try and forget. It is best to forget!'*

There will come a time to forget.

These dark details are not being compiled for the sake of it; they are to let her know she is not alone. For she will have to bear the burden of what is to come.

My darling girl, my angel – for that is what she is, despite being born into such hell: his land; his house; a marriage forced upon me. One child, but there will be no more. His hand will never touch me in that way again, I will make sure of it. If only I were stronger; if only I could bear this burden instead of she – but it is not to be.

There are things one should never see, not here, not in this realm; that should never be allowed to cross the great divide. But they *will* cross, if you goad them, if you taunt them, if, above all you offer them sanctuary. A devout Christian is how he portrays himself, and how he fools those around him with his supposedly pious ways. Such a pillar of the community! So benevolent! But he has never fooled me. I could see the darkness in him from our very first meeting and I shrank back because of it. He saw something in me too – not a shining heart, a girl to love, not even innocence, for in so many ways this gift erodes that. What he saw was someone he thought he could mould, and so he pursued me, he *hounded* me – his supposed wealth and power blinding my otherwise loving parents. I was handed over as a prized animal might be handed over: to the slaughter.

And now I am a mother…

I look up. The door is rattling, the handle turning, first one way, and then the other; not a frenzied action, not yet, but soon it will be. It is not him, nor the maid or the housekeeper, for they will not venture into the attic either. They have no need.

It is one of *them*, seeking to stop me; desperate to do so. Ignorance is such a powerful thing; it gives the idle an excuse to follow, to bend the knee, to be led. It is the ignorant who will summon those from across the gulf that exists to divide us. If only they realised more fully what they were doing; what it is that they unleash.

I am not ignorant. I do know. And what is on the other side of the door *hates* that I do. These things – for I refuse to name them – are the very embodiment of hate.

But they will not enter either. In here I have spun a light, one that has nothing to do with the sun or the moon and that will never fade. I have built a wall so high I can no longer see over the top. It protects me, but more than that, it protects what is now written. It will hide these pages should they ever manage to enter. It will block them.

In the end it will block everything.

Such is the price I must pay.

Darling Rosamund, my greatest wish is that you – and only you – unearth what lies buried, and when you do, may it help you to find a way through hell.

Do not despair. Be strong, far stronger than I have been.

I am sorry at having borne you into this. At least I will not bear another.

This is why I write. Not to save myself, but to save you.

Chapter One

Fourteen Years Later

"ROSAMUND! Rosamund! Where are you?"

With the tiled floor cold against my stockinged feet, I flew down the length of the corridor as far from that voice as possible. The narrow walls on either side of me were covered in floral wallpaper, not bright in colour, and not cheerful either, rather it looked as if a thousand tiny flowers were caught in various stages of decay. It was only I that ever used this corridor, although it was one of many in this house, which, beside myself, only my father, a housekeeper and a maid occupied. A house set miles from towns and villages, from *life*, concealed deep in the countryside.

Father was not always in residence, spending a great deal of his time in London, mixing no doubt with other eminent landowners born into riches. I was glad he was rarely home. My father and I were not close; I make this known from the outset. There was *no one* in the house to whom I was close. The new maid, Josie, was proving to be an elusive creature, and Miss Tiggs, the housekeeper, who seemed to have been here forever, certainly since my birth, disliked me as much as I disliked her. There did not appear to be a particular reason for our mutual dislike but for my part, I found her... peculiar, keeping to the kitchens as she did, her domain, as I have always thought of it. I once had a governess, but I had not seen her in months and no one thought this odd, least of all my father, who, when I saw fit to remark upon her absence, shut me up with a stern 'Can you not see I'm busy? I am reading.'

When home, when not in search of me, he usually locked himself away in his study, on which occasions I could imagine well enough the concentration on his foxlike face as he waded through the tomes that lined the shelves there. When he grew weary of the books, however, he would demand I sit with him, his whisky-soured breath potent as he asked me the same question over and over. *What do you see?*

I did not wish to play such a tiresome game today; to gaze deep into his eyes, as dark as mine, as they continued to narrow and hunt for any information I might be able to impart. The moment I heard him roar, I glanced towards the clock on the mantelpiece of my bedroom. It was early; barely midday. Surely he was not imbibing already? Frightened that his summons meant something; that he was angry in some way, distressed or disturbed, I tore myself from my book – for I loved to read too – and picked up my skirts and ran, through labyrinthine corridors, past empty rooms, barely glancing at the rain-drenched Sussex landscape outside.

I had been doing this ever since I could remember: running. Sixteen now and no longer a child, I was practically a young woman, but running seemed to have been as much an integral part of my life as the mutual dislike between myself and Miss Tiggs; a simple *fact* of it. Was I indeed frightened when he came for me? Sometimes.

At other times I was angered by it – especially if engrossed in a particular passage in a book, or involved in the painting of a watercolour, depicting the misty grounds of the house perhaps, or its rather grand Georgian exterior. Mears House was where I resided. No one had ever explained to me why it was christened as such; whether indeed it was a Mears family that lived there originally, or if it was named for the architect that built it. Certainly, it seemed to have no connection to my family name, that of Howard. I sketched the house quite often: nine windows plus the grand door with a portico dominating the front elevation. I also painted the grounds in which it sits; the grass and the countless trees that form a ring of woodland around the house, in which only I ever seemed to roam. I would draw the path in front of the house, the one that meandered through the landscape, which I longed to run down, away from here and into a world I could only imagine. And, of course, I would draw the roof with only one window at the rear to punctuate the expanse of grey slate – not nearly enough to benefit such an attic. I imagined there should have been more, if only for the sake of symmetry.

The attic was a safe place for me. I had no idea why Father would not venture there. I knew only that once he had taken the right turn at the rear of the house that led to another much narrower flight of stairs, one I always regarded as hidden, he would come to an abrupt halt. Only once had he dared to stand outside the attic door; to touch the handle, tentatively, testing it this way and that, almost pushing it open before deciding against it and retreating. The relief that I had felt!

I held no such reservation and having reached the attic

myself, I closed the door behind me, stopping at last to catch my breath from the steep climb. As I have previously noted, it is a vast room, not entirely covering the length and breadth of the house, but within the attic, it did feel so. In many ways it seemed *bigger* than the house. There were discarded boxes everywhere and items of furniture covered in white sheets that, in the gloom from the single distant window, were capable of casting the oddest of shapes, conjuring people with twisted limbs. According to my former governess, I had always had an overactive imagination! The attic was not overly dark as the daylight from that intrepid window filtered well enough through the cobwebs. What would it be like with no sunlight at all, however, and no moon glow either? Perhaps then there would be reason enough to be frightened.

"Rosamund!"

Still I could hear him. No doubt he was at the bottom of those hidden stairs, standing with fists clenched, his lips a thin white line.

As I looked around, I tried to understand: why would he not come up here? What was it that repelled him? I would pay for being disobedient in due course, for not coming to heel as a dog might. If only I could hide in this lofty space forever, but I could not. I would have to resurface. And when I did, he would drag me to his study, push me back into that cracked and worn leather chair that stood across the desk from his, and growl at me until I succumbed; until I gave him at least some semblance of an answer. *What do you see?*

Not wishing to think of my fate, I weaved around the furniture, my tread careful as I made my way to the far end of the room, to where the hazy light shone like candlelight through gossamer, so softly. There was a desk there, positioned in an alcove; a small one, the kind that may have been used in a school I tended to think, although I had never been to one, but I had certainly seen sketches of such institutions in books. Fine places they looked, with so many others just like me – children that may have become friends. How wonderful to have had a friend.

Or a mother.

As I took my seat at the desk; as my shoulders slumped and my head fell forwards in despair, I forced myself to take more deep breaths. I would not cry. I refused to. In my current reading matter – aptly named *Bleak House* by Mr Charles Dickens – was a character described as a 'plucky little thing'. That is what I now aspired to be – plucky. But, oh, how I missed Mother. Strange, considering I had no living memory of her, that in this house there was nothing that even alluded to her. Certainly, Father never mentioned her name; would *never even* have her mentioned.

I remember when I had tried.

"Father, was Mother kind? Was she gentle? Were her eyes as dark as mine? What happened to her, Father? You have never really told me. How did she die?"

Perhaps it had been wrong to act in such a manner, firing question after question at him. Shadows had darkened his face and his nostrils had flared. Could he really be blamed for losing his temper, for shouting at me, for screaming?

"Stop plaguing me, child! I can stand no more of your infernal curiosity. Where is Miss Lyons? Where is she? Why am I paying her such a handsome fee?"

Miss Lyons was the governess, missing as my mother

was missing; 'gone home to London' apparently, 'for she's 'ad her fill of you too,' that last tidbit told to me by Miss Tiggs, a cruel smile on her dough-like face as she delivered such harsh words.

On that day my father had wanted to cast me from him, into the hands of Miss Lyons, rather than seeking me out – it was always about extremes with Father.

And now I must hasten to correct myself. I have said that there was no trace of Mother in this house, beside myself, her progeny; but I *had* found something; something that he knew nothing about. And I kept it safe. I kept it here, in the attic.

It was a photograph of her, just her and no one else. In it she wears a dark dress. It is impossible to tell the colour of it, as it simply appears black in the photograph, just as her hair appears black, coiled around her head. Her eyes are dark too, but her skin… it is as pale as milk. The dress is high-collared but around her neck there hangs a necklace, one hand resting below it, her long slim fingers artfully curled, although one, the index finger, is elongated, as though it points to the necklace. She has about her a wistful quality, and behind her is a curious, almost luminous light.

The photograph lay inside the desk. Opening the lid, I retrieved it, moving further into the light in order to study it. It was found in the library, my favourite room in a house I could otherwise not abide. Put there by Mother herself? Did she want someone to find it, and specifically me, her daughter? As I held it in my hand that was the feeling it conveyed, as if her mouth was far from closed but whispering: *Remember me. I did exist.*

The photograph had been guarded between a book by

Charlotte Brontë called *Jane Eyre* – a book I adored about another 'plucky' character, Jane herself – and *Songs of Innocence and Experience* by the poet William Blake, that I had yet to read. Had Mother known I would love reading so much? It was not difficult to guess at, I supposed. In this house, so far removed from everything, reading and drawing constituted full-time occupations. When I chose *Jane Eyre* and the photograph fell to the floor, I was amazed. Setting the book down on a nearby table, I studied the picture. The feeling I mentioned earlier – that she wanted to be recognised – engulfed me. Although no name was scribed on the back – although I appeared to look more like my father than her – this was, without doubt, Mother. She had hidden it here; she had wanted me to gaze upon her.

If Father knew what I had in my possession, what it was I *could* see right now... I did not care, for she was the only thing I wanted to see.

*Oh, Mother, I might look like Father, but it is you I take after in all other aspects. Say it is so. Please. I do not want to be like him. He is everything I aspire **not** to be.*

If only she would speak.

A movement a few feet away captured my attention and stopped me from sliding further into melancholy. What was it? A spider? A rat? I hoped it was not the latter as I had a fear of them with their bead-like eyes and their sharp, pointed teeth. I was not so fond of spiders either, especially the big leggy ones that scurried rather than ran along the corridors of Mears House. I stood up and stamped my feet hard against the floorboards, noting a slight loosening of one as I did so, and quickly sidestepping it. If it was a rat, such actions should be enough to deter it from drawing closer.

But still there was movement.

Persistent movement.

A stirring and a rustling.

I braced myself as I continued to stare at the corner where the noise was coming from, remembering my father's words.

What do you see?

Chapter Two

"IT is madness, William! Sheer madness!"

The voice of the friend that had come visiting, unlike Father's quiet, almost whispery conversational voice, was bellowing. It was *his* friend, of course, not mine. As I have stated, I had none. How could I, when I was confined to Mears House? Soon other friends would arrive to gather in his study. They would smoke cigars and drink whisky, venturing further into discussion as I lingered here, at the far end of the corridor, hiding behind a door that led into the drawing room – one of the three reception rooms the house boasted – trying to listen to what it was that they had to say.

Of course they did not limit their assemblies to here, as I was sure they congregated in London too, because that is where most of them hailed from. I knew this because I had overheard them discuss their places of residence on several occasions; suburbs such as Knightsbridge and Hammersmith, Highgate and Chelsea, which I envisaged to be outrageously grand places with buildings that towered over you and a fine assortment of ladies and gentlemen parading on the streets or galloping along in carriages. I was under no illusion London was entirely grand; I understood it had its dark side too – Mr Dickens had made that clear enough. There appeared to be a dark side to everything and perhaps in turn, everyone. When I thought of Mr Dickens' London, I imagined a thick blanket of fog enveloping it – the 'London Particular' as Mr Guppy in *Bleak House* tells Miss Summerson; a real pea souper, worse than anything we have ever had in the countryside. The city I pictured was both a den of magnificence and inequity, smog lending it an otherworldly air, and I longed to visit this mystical and terrible land; to experience it for myself rather than through the eyes of an author.

My father's visitors travelled by horse and carriage to Mears House and were furtively deposited on the gravel path outside, their means of transport quickly disappearing into the distance. Almost always they stayed the night. The moment they retired was when I would stop eavesdropping, pick up my skirts and run once again, this time to my bedroom. Once inside I would push a chest of drawers up against the door, heaving with all my might for it was a solid piece of furniture, just in case one of the gentlemen should decide to go wandering in the night and become disorientated, and I would find the handle of my door turning, always turning…

But for now I listened, filled with curiosity. Just what was 'sheer madness'?

"It's just… There is danger," the friend continued. "What if it should go wrong?"

"You have now changed your mind?" my father questioned.

"For God's sake, William, acknowledge the risks involved at least!"

My father laughed, but I could detect no humour in it. When he spoke again, his voice was so low it forced me to leave my hiding space and creep forward to hear.

"You are aware that there are many, many men that would willingly take your place, who would give their eye teeth for such an opportunity?"

After a moment of silence, Arthur coughed. "I am merely saying—"

"Courage is required, Arthur, not cowardice."

Arthur was clearly considering the warning in Father's voice. "Are you sure she is able to assist us?" he said at last.

I was merely a step or two away from the door now, my hand cupping my ear as I strained to hear. *Who* were they talking of?

"Arthur, I am certain of it."

"There will not be a repeat of what happened previously?"

"You are right, sir, there will not."

Another voice startled me.

"Miss, is there something I can help you with?"

I swung around. In front of me was the maid – not quite so elusive now – her expression perplexed. In my estimation I was younger than Josie by two or three years, but I was the mistress of this house, *her* mistress, and so I straightened my back and my chin too, refusing to be embarrassed at being caught out by a servant.

"Thank you, but I am quite comfortable. Is there anything I can help *you* with?"

She shrugged – an insolent gesture I could not help but think, or was it? Was it that she was just a simple girl, an untroubled girl? For in the few times I had encountered her, not scurrying around the house as I scurried, or as the spiders scurried, but 'drifting' around it, she had looked so serene and contented. Strangely, she had also looked at home. How long had she been with us? A matter of months, replacing Lottie who left to marry a cousin twice removed from the West Country. Time in this house, however, could not be trusted. It was something of an anomaly, either passing by in a moment, or stretching on before you with no end in sight. Josie carried out her various duties in a world seemingly of her own making, often remaining just on the edge of vision; but now she was in full view and staring at me.

The time was three o' clock, the month November. Soon the already weakening light of winter would fade entirely to be replaced by a darkness so complete it would require effort to see your own hands held up in front of your face. I had read that eyes take some minutes to adjust to such intense darkness, but in my experience that was not always true, for the darkness could remain that way – intense – right up until morning. There was much for Josie to do before the arrival of Father's other friends, yet still she gawped at me.

"Josie," I asked, breaking the silence that seemed to have settled so heavily upon us, "is everything well? I asked if there was something I could help you with?"

"Oh no, miss. I don't think so."

Her amusement, or rather *bemusement,* failed to amuse me.

"Everything is prepared for Father's guests? The beds have been turned down?"

"Everything's prepared," she accompanied that statement with an enthusiastic nod, causing wisps of red-tinged hair to fall from under her cap.

"Miss Tiggs has supper ready?"

"Just a light supper's been requested, miss."

Of course it had! They would be light on eating, heavy

on drinking.

The way Josie continued to look at me made me feel like some sort of oddity. Perturbed, I had to struggle to retain my composure. Turning my back on her, I retraced my footsteps along the corridor, back to the drawing room.

"The grate in here," I called, intending to lead her to it, "I noticed it still had embers in it earlier. Why is this? It is supposed to be raked out every morning."

I turned my head just enough to see her smile slip.

"I'm sorry, miss, It's just…I've been so busy…"

"Busy staring is what it seems."

I disliked the sound of my own voice, it reminded me too much of Father's, but, as I have pointed out, I was the mistress of this house, despite my tender years. Perhaps this was how I was *required* to sound – not acerbic, not exactly, but authoritative at least. During Father's absence, I was in charge of this… this… mausoleum; it seemed such an apt word to describe it. As Josie's smile had slipped, something inside me followed suit. It was just so dreary in here, so lacklustre, with paint peeling on every ceiling and the wallpaper fading. When rarely the light crept in, it did so halfheartedly.

I faced her fully now. "Why do you stay? Why do you not leave? You have family, so why not return to them?"

Josie's green eyes widened and I understood why. How could I have let such desperate words escape me? But there was such a longing in me to know; a need. "*Do* you have family, Josie? A mother?"

"Everyone has a mother."

About to rebuke her for being so insensitive – surely she was fully aware of my situation – I managed to stop myself. Firstly, I had asked the question and so there must be a reply, and secondly, she was right, everyone did have a mother. *I* had a mother, or rather a photograph of her.

I hung my head, my own hair, brown in colour, not restrained, not today, but falling forwards to frame my face. "Why do you stay?" I asked again.

"I…" she was tentative now, nervous at last. "I like it here."

I was incredulous. "You like it? Why?"

"It's quiet."

"Quiet?"

"On occasion."

Before I could query that too, she continued. "I have my own bed."

"Your own bed?" I seemed doomed to repeat her words.

"At home, there are nine of us, and only two beds."

And that was it, the sole reason. This was a girl whose own bed – her own space I supposed – meant everything. Was it no more complex than that?

From outside there came the crunch of carriage wheels on gravel and, like co-conspirators now, we both took a step towards the window so that we could cautiously peer onto the driveway. There were more guests arriving and no doubt Miss Tiggs would escort them straight to Father's study and wait on them throughout the evening. She was the only female allowed access to the inner-sanctum at these times – Miss Tiggs with her doughface and her cruel smile. We watched them alight. There were two of them, an older man and a younger one with fair hair. The former was quite stooped, the latter straight-backed, handsome even, with a somewhat confident gait. Having deposited them, the carriage turned swiftly around and sped back down the approach, eager as always to put as much distance between it and the house as possible. As I watched it, I recalled snatches of Father and Arthur's conversation.

'Madness, sheer madness' and *'Are you sure she is able to assist us?'*

Once again I wondered, who was this 'she' they talked of?

Chapter Three

FATHER'S associates had returned to London, but surprisingly he had stayed at Mears House. I had not foreseen this, as it was far more usual that he should leave with them, and so I had risen later than normal, shooing Josie away when she appeared at my door to tend to me. I had failed to sleep well the previous night; I never did when Father's gentlemen friends stayed over, and what sleep I had managed was filled with such strangeness, such turmoil, that my eyes frequently snapped open as my mouth gaped, fish-like, for air; and yet, in the cold light of day, I could barely recall the hazy, twisted shapes that had caused such angst. In truth, I had no desire to recall them, but there would be torment ahead for me regardless – that caused by my Father.

Breakfast had already been taken in the dining room, where I had sat alone as usual, staring idly out of the windows at yet another rain-swept day, the colours outside matching the sombreness of those inside. It threatened to be one of those endless days, but at least, besides Miss Tiggs and Josie, I had the house to myself – or so I believed.

"There you are!"

I was passing his study on my way to the drawing room, intent on doing some reading perhaps beside the fire, or to indulge in a little drawing. Although I was not having any tuition at the time at least my past governesses – for Miss Lyons was only one of them – had taught me sufficiently in both respects.

"Father!" On spotting him, my voice was little more than a croak. "But I thought you had gone." Or rather I had *hoped* he would be gone; that I was rid of him.

"Several times I have called for you," he declared, "in vain, I might add."

"Perhaps I was out walking, Father," I lied. "I do enjoy being outside, even in the rain." Another lie, I was wary of the rain as my chest tended towards weakness.

Father made no reply, he simply stared at me – again he reminded me of a fox with his intent, narrow gaze and features that jutted and jarred. His dark eyes were infinite pools that mesmerised and tethered: I had to fight against this, not look away – Father would deem such an act insufferable rudeness on my part – but not lose myself in them. I cursed that I resembled him; in truth I despaired of it.

"Come to my study," he said at last, not asking but demanding.

My heart plummeted further – why oh why must we do this? What did he want from me? How was I to answer the oddest of questions that fell from his lips? I am just a girl, an ordinary girl – his *daughter* – why did he interrogate me so?

I have mentioned that, besides the library, Father's study harboured books too, many of them lining the length and breadth of three entire walls. As much as I loved books, in Father's room they failed to furnish it; rather they gave it a closed-in claustrophobic feel and made it so much darker than it already was. They were not storybooks either; Father held no regard for the frivolity of fiction. No, these were books pertaining to lofty scientific subjects such as astronomy, physics and medicine. Some of them had titles and text in Latin, and once, when he had left me alone in his study for a short while, I had made a closer examination of them, running my fingers up and down their crumbling leather spines. And oh, the feelings that had overwhelmed me as I had done so! The visions that had begun to form in my mind…

"Sit down." Again it was a command, thrown at me from over his shoulder as he stalked to his own chair. How I wished I could be 'plucky' and continue to stand, to ask why it was he always commanded, why we could never just converse.

The air reeked of stale whisky and tobacco, one managing to dominate for a few seconds before the other fought to take over. Velvet curtains at the window – burgundy in colour but far from opulent owing to their almost decrepit state – were barely pulled apart, keeping the daylight deliberately at bay. I had to battle to keep my breathing steady as I hated to show Father I was frightened. More than that, I hated to admit it to myself. If only I had the picture of Mother to cling to, but she was in the attic, safe from discovery.

As he sank onto his chair, he leaned back, clasping his hands together and landing them on the deep red leather of his desktop. There were several books within arms' reach, perhaps those that had been referenced recently by himself and his acquaintances. They were not neatly placed, as I tended to place mine on the side table in my room or on the desk in the library, but strewn in a haphazard manner. Also on the desk there was an inkpot, a pen and some notes, illegible perhaps except to the scribe, for certainly the scrawl seemed chaotic as well. All this I took in over the course of seconds, bracing myself; suppressing any rising panic.

Father surprised me with what he said next.

"You need a new wardrobe of clothes."

I inclined my head to the side. "Clothes, Father?"

"Yes," he replied, no smile upon his face, indeed his expression was sombre.

"An assortment of dresses, a new coat and a shawl. Your boots are scuffed. Goodness knows what you kick at all day. You will need to replace them as well."

"Clothes?" I said again, beginning to feel a curious stirring in the pit of my stomach – could it be excitement? "But, Father, where am I to buy such clothes?"

"London."

"London?"

"Of course, where else would one go but London?"

I could barely believe the evidence of my own ears. I had entered Father's study expecting the usual bombardment of questions, but instead was being offered the most incredible of opportunities! I was to leave Mears House – actually *leave* here – and travel to London; witness with my own eyes the carriages that pounded the cobbled streets; the fancy men, women, and children that lived there.

"Am I to go with you, Father?"

"I will accompany you, yes."

"But how will I know where to go, and where shall we stay? It is such a long way, surely we cannot be travelling to and fro on the same day?"

Abruptly, Father stood up, his nostrils flaring. "Questions, questions. You are always so full of questions,

Rosamund!"

I took a moment to digest that statement, or rather the irony of it. Was it not always *he* that asked the questions – questions I did not know how to *begin* to answer. *What do you see?* I shall tell you – just as I told him on so many occasions. I saw the world around me, which comprised four crumbling walls and a series of rooms that lay empty, nothing within them but dust motes which performed a frenzied dance in the air should one happen to disturb them. Outside there was endless grass; a sky that tended only towards blue in the summer and a collection of tall trees that encircled us; that formed a barrier almost, only permitting a choice few into its realm, but mostly guilty of keeping others away. That is *exactly* what I saw but soon, if Father was to be believed, I would be seeing something else too.

Determined to hold onto the excitement of the moment rather than give in to intimidation, I took a deep breath and pressed further with my concerns. "Father, I have never been to London before, as you know, and I am certain that Josie—"

"Arthur's daughter has agreed to be your guide."

"Arthur's daughter?" Had he not just heard what I had just said?

"That is correct. Her name escapes me, what is it?" He huffed and puffed for a few seconds before clicking his fingers. "Constance, there it is."

"Arthur is one of the gentlemen that visited yesterday evening?" I knew this to be true, but what Father forgets is that I have never been introduced to any of them.

"Yes, yes," was his reply, and again there was that annoyance; that implication that I had no right to question anything.

As he started to wear the carpet beneath his feet with his constant pacing – Father always did this, as if he could never rest, not for long – I noticed something else, something that perhaps had not fully registered until now. Father was *impeccably* dressed. There was no need for him to be entirely outfitted. His black thigh-length jacket covered a waistcoat and trousers that were cut from the same cloth, the waistcoat boasting ivory buttons, and his white shirt with its tall collar was perfectly starched. On his feet were boots that either Miss Tiggs or Josie had polished so well you could see your own reflection in them. He cut a dapper figure; another word I had learnt courtesy of Mr Dickens. I glanced down at my own attire and realised how much I looked like a poor relation rather than the daughter of a moneyed landowner. The dress I was wearing was slightly too small for me, as all my dresses were, every stitch doing its duty. However, it was not only me that was shabby; something else was too.

I swallowed slightly before taking yet another breath.

"Father, should we... Is it right...?"

Coming to a grinding halt, Father turned his head towards me, such a swift, jagged action that for a moment I was reminded of dreams I would prefer to forget.

"Spit it out, Rosamund," he insisted, although it was he who was guilty of spitting.

"It is just..." Still I struggled to find the right words, but once begun, I had to finish. "If there is money, should we not spend it on the house?"

As soon as my sentence was complete I realised my mistake.

"*If* there is money?" he repeated.

Breathe, Rosamund, continue to breathe.

Pitifully, I gestured around me. "There is a leak in my bedroom ceiling, I noticed it last night. I will have a bucket put in there to catch the drips, but also, in the dining room, there is mould in several corners, and in the drawing room that I frequent—"

He was by my side in an instant, his breath scalding my cheek as he grabbed my shoulders. "Are you questioning my solvency?"

"No… I… The house…"

"The management of my financial affairs has nothing to do with you. Question me again and it will be at your peril."

"Yes, Father. Sorry, Father."

"You will do as you are told."

"Yes."

"As *I* tell you."

"Of course, Father."

"You are to be seen, Rosamund. *Seen!* And look at you! You are no better than an urchin that haunts the dark alleys and streets of the city that we are to visit."

"An urchin? I meant no ill—"

My desperate attempts to appease him fell short. He held me still and, as though I was caught in a vice, there was no escape. Try as I might I could not look away or refuse to stare deeper into those eyes of his – his gaze captured me, it *seared* me. And in it, there was no love, not a hint. Nor was there any mercy.

Chapter Four

THE trip to London was postponed. Further into the day that Father had sprung such glorious news upon me, I had begun to sniffle. By the following day, I had fully developed a head cold. Father acted as if I had become deliberately ill. Quite how he could think so was beyond me as I was *desperate* to escape this house. The very next day, however, he left without even saying goodbye, leaving me with just Miss Tiggs and Josie to nurse me – and of the two, Miss Tiggs kept her distance, as she always did. I presumed he had gone to London, but for how long this time I had no idea. Sometimes it was just days; at other times he would be gone for well over a week, more rarely two. I experienced the usual relief at his departure, but now, for the first time, there was also a touch of dismay. Sincerely, I hoped I had not ruined my chances to accompany him in the future.

London. How I had dreamed of it! How I had wanted to be a part of it! Society: it was such a glorious word, so full of life and magnificence compared to the word I would choose to describe my current circumstance: isolated. As I lay on the sofa in the drawing room, I do not recall ever feeling so adrift. Beside me on a long low table, my books lay untouched; my sketchpad too, a collection of lead pencils looking somewhat forlorn beside it. I had quite a collection of pencils and sketchpads, this being the one avenue in which Father would indulge me, seemingly keen that I should spend my time sketching. Occasionally he took my scribbles from me and kept them in his study. I wished to think it a sign of affection that he should be so interested, but in truth it was merely self-delusion.

Why had Mother loved him so, if she ever really did? Could he have been different as a young man, when she was alive and breathing beside him? Did losing his wife and being left with a baby to tend affect him so deeply that it changed his character? Was he handsome once as she was pretty? Just as there were no photographs of Mother in the house save for the one I had in my possession, there were no photographs of him either, or indeed myself. This house, with its stark walls and its aura of sorrowfulness, was a house held in a moment; that moment being despair.

I sensed someone else in the drawing room beside myself. I turned my head to look, not quickly, but slowly, feeling strangely unnerved.

"Oh, Josie," I said on a release of breath. "It is you!"

"Of course, miss, who else could it be?"

Perhaps because I was feeling so unwell – my chest tight, my head pounding, my nose sore – that I grew instantly irritated. "For goodness sake, must you creep up on me like that? I would prefer that you knocked on the door before entering."

"Oh," Josie replied, looking instantly stricken. How pale she was; such a delicate creature, slighter than myself and I had barely any flesh to boast of. "I'm sorry, miss. I did knock, honest I did. When you didn't answer—"

"You thought you would walk right in."

"I thought it'd be empty, miss. Often it is."

Insolence! She was so insolent!

To my amazement she did not cower further, but continued walking towards me, a bucket in her hand, one that contained more wood for the fire. It looked very heavy to me, but she managed it well enough. She was clearly stronger than her appearance suggested. Dropping to her knees, she placed a fresh log upon the grate, and immediately flames sprang up around it, growing higher and higher.

"It's cold in here," she murmured.

"It is cold in all the rooms," I snapped. "Even in summer there is a chill throughout this house."

"Is that why you're prone to head colds, miss, because it's so chilly?"

"Prone?" I was already wearing a frown but it deepened. "How do you know that I am prone to head colds?" As far as I could recall I had succumbed to only one since Josie's arrival, and it had been far less tiresome than this present one.

There was that shrug again. "I just wondered, that's all."

After placing the bucket by the side of the fire, she stood, smoothing her apron with her now free hands. "Can I get you something to eat, miss? There's a cheese flan in the pantry, I can fetch you a slice if you wish."

"No thank you, I have no appetite."

"Another warm drink?"

Another? I had not yet been offered a first!

"That would be nice."

"Some lemon and honey in water? It'll help to soothe your throat."

"Yes, thank you, Josie. Ask Miss Tiggs—"

"No need. I'll make it. I know how. I used to make it often enough at home."

Having informed me of this, Josie smiled and again I was startled – it contained such brilliance, such enthusiasm. Any irritation of mine that lingered was wiped away immediately, and despite how wretched I felt, I found myself smiling back at her, although I could not match such brilliance.

Hastening to her task, she turned to go, taking a few steps before coming to a stop. She was gazing at something on the table, my books perhaps? I followed her line of sight and it led not towards the books, but to my sketchpad, which was lying open at a depiction of Mears House, as viewed from the gardens.

"Josie? Is it the drawing you are looking at?"

She nodded rather than answered.

"Do you like to draw too?" I asked.

It was a wry smile that graced her face this time. "I don't have time to draw, miss." Before I could reply further, she shifted her gaze and stared at me instead. "It's a very good drawing," she somewhat grandly informed me. "Interesting."

My tone was irritated again as I leant over and closed the sketchpad. "I am delighted it meets with your approval."

"Is that how you see it, this house?"

My frown returned. "Of course this is how I see it. This is how it is."

"When you're better, I should like to accompany you for a walk in the grounds."

"A walk?" I choked on such an offer, my cough rendering me quite incapable of further speech.

"Yes," she said before taking her leave, "so that we can see the house together."

* * *

It was practically a full week after my conversation with Josie in the drawing room that I felt well enough to take in some fresh air. I had no intention of walking with her, however. I would simply do as I had always done and meander alone throughout the grounds, making it as far as the trees perhaps and disappearing for a while into the shelter of the woods.

After breakfast, I fetched my coat from the cloakroom – a threadbare thing really, that barely lent enough warmth – and returned to the hall and the front door, having to pull with both hands to open it. As soon as the door yielded, a blast of cold air hit me, causing me to momentarily reconsider my intent, but then as I inhaled and my lungs filled with the lightness and thinness of the winter morning, I realised just how much I had been craving something fresh. Stepping outside with renewed vigour, I shut the door, pushed my gloved hands into my pockets and, with my head down, began to walk, quickly veering off the gravel pathway and onto the grass. I should like to record that the lawns surrounding Mears House were well tended, green and lush, but the truth is they were as neglected as the house; as neglected as I myself. Not words of self-pity, I assure you, just the plain truth.

Walking with Josie indeed! What a notion! Then again, perhaps I should attempt to ask Father a second time if she could accompany me to London. Surely I needed a maid, if only for the sake of appearance. If Josie could not come, I would be entirely at the mercy of Constance. What would she be like, I wondered, this mystery woman? Kind and pretty or intolerant of my naivety? Would we walk together, arm in arm through the busy and vibrant streets, or would I have to shuffle behind her like a poor relation while she marched ahead with all the confidence of familiarity?

Cease being so negative, Rosamund, she will act like a lady, as must you.

I may have had my misgivings but still I could not help but giggle with excitement, wrapping my arms around me as I continued to walk onwards.

Finally, I reached the trees, grateful indeed for their shelter as the wind had now picked up and was beginning to cause my chest to ache again. Instead of grass beneath my scuffed boots, now I could hear the crunch of crisp dead leaves vying with the squelch of mud. It is quiet in the woods, peaceful. As in the attic, I felt I had entered a different place where only I existed. Myself and… nature. Yes, that was it, only natural things.

Pushing my hair from my eyes, I raised my head. The house was in sight, distant but no less vast because of that. It was far too big for the four of us that inhabited it. Josie's numerous brothers and sisters could have had a room each, not just a bed!

My bedroom was at the rear, and therefore north facing, as was the lone attic window. Sometimes I would go to the rear of the house and stand there, to do what I was doing now – examine it. I fancied the windows were like eyes, so many of them, staring back at me – the house not made of bricks and mortar but something more sentient.

I gasped.

Who was that at the window of one of the reception rooms, not the one I usually occupied, but a different one? Whoever it was had raised their hands to the glass.

It was Josie of course; she must have noticed me, just as I had noticed her.

Was she waving? If so, why was she doing so with both hands? The action seemed rather desperate.

Tentatively, I raised my hand and started to wave back. The moment I did that, her waving abruptly stopped. I shook my head in confusion before briefly closing my eyes, and when I opened them, the figure had gone. Vanished. I blinked and blinked, but there was to be no reappearance. I resolved to ask Josie later what she meant by it; whether she was indeed distressed or simply playing an odd sort of game.

The cold defeating me, I decided to retreat back to Mears House. The last thing I wanted was to risk a relapse of my illness. When Father returned home, I wanted to be fit and well to greet him, and encourage him to take me away from here. There would be no more mention of finances, and no more concern on my part about the subject either. As Father had said, it was his responsibility, not mine.

Re-entering the house, I made my way to the drawing room, there to pass the afternoon and doze intermittently. Whenever I awoke the fire was always blazing, although there was no sign of Josie tending to it. Still, I felt happy enough, the warmth succeeding in making the room almost cosy. As night fell, I realised how hungry I had become. Rising, I made my way to the kitchen, looking out for Josie but not encountering her. Venturing past

Father's study, I saw the door was firmly shut, whilst other doors remained either slightly ajar or fully open. I tutted. During winter, doors should always remain closed in Mears House in order to prevent what little warmth there was from escaping. I have instructed Josie on this point several times, so why did she refuse to listen? If I saw her in the kitchen, I would have to tell her yet again.

The kitchen door was shut at least. I stood before it, wondering whether to knock. Quickly, I shook my head. Why should I? This was my house. *Out of courtesy, Rosamund, common courtesy.* Grudgingly I had to agree with my better self. Courtesy should be extended to include everyone, even the likes of Miss Tiggs.

Determined to stifle the butterflies in my stomach – they always started to flutter when I was in this part of the house – I knocked on the door.

"Enter," a voice from within commanded. How imperious she sounded and how ill at ease I felt as a consequence. *But I am the mistress of this house!*

I clutched the door handle, turned it and strode in, my head held high and my back straight. And there she was, by the fire, barely lifting her head to glance my way, a mug of something in her hands, ale I would wager, for it seemed to be her favourite tipple. For a moment I felt like screaming at her: *where is my dinner?*

"Miss Tiggs," my voice was impressively calm, "I should like something to eat."

"You hungry?"

"Yes, yes. Of course I am. It is dinnertime. Past dinnertime, in fact. Why has no one called for me?"

"Why'd ya think?"

From the way she was slurring her words it was clear

she was drunk, hence why she was babbling and why there was no dinner available. Could I really blame her, though? I rather think I envied her. Alcohol seemed to blur the edges, thus making the solitariness of Mears House perhaps easier to bear.

"I should like something to eat," I repeated. "Nothing elaborate, just some bread will do, some cheese and some ham if we have it."

Rather than rise from her chair, she nodded towards the larder. "In there," she muttered.

"Am I to fetch it myself?" I said, incredulous.

"You 'ave before now."

She was right, I had. In fact, just lately it was becoming more and more common, as was finding her in this state, slumped by the fire, having supped too well if not wisely, her hands forever clinging to that mug. I supposed I could have argued the point with this excuse for a housekeeper, but I decided against it. She was old, well into her sixties, her body as doughy as her face. Let her sit, let her sup, I was perfectly capable, and at least I could rest assured that the hands which touched my food – my own – were clean. Sometimes the grime beneath her fingernails made me shudder.

Having filled a plate, I took a seat at a small dining table a few feet from the fire.

"You 'aving it 'ere?" she said, observing me.

"Yes, I will not be long."

"Up to you, I s'pose," she muttered, shifting her weight and groaning.

"It would be nice to have a dog, would it not?"

I do not even now know what made me say such a thing, but suddenly I had a yearning for such a creature to inhabit this house – a companion that would have raised its head when I walked in; indeed would have left the solace of the fireside because its need to be petted and fussed by me outweighed everything.

"Your father won't countenance a dog," was all Miss Tiggs said in response. "And neither will I, not 'ere, in the kitchen. Filthy things they are."

Filthy? And yet the smell that emitted from Miss Tiggs was often eye-watering!

As I ate I tried again to make conversation.

"I am to go to London, you know. Father said so."

"Oh?'

"Yes, I am to get an entire new wardrobe of clothes, because I am to be seen, by society, I mean. I am to be presented."

A snort escaped her, followed by a short sharp cough.

"Well, I am looking forward to it," I said, munching on cheese that tasted sour.

"When's he back?"

He? "Mr Howard, you mean?"

"Of course, Mr Howard!"

"Presently," I said, seething at her lack of respect.

"So, you're going soon?"

"Apparently so."

"Good," she muttered, her head nodding. "About time."

I could not help but agree. "I may take Josie with me."

She looked at me then. "Oh, you might, might you?"

"Yes," I said, haughty again. "I think I shall."

"If you can find her."

"Where is she?" I asked.

"You tell me."

Goodness, what I had to put with in this house! It was insufferable.

I took another bite of my meal. If the cheese was sour, the bread was worse, hard at the edges, and the ham was bland, in need of a pickle or a chutney to give it substance. But there were no such fancies in the larder, only the basics.

In response, I saw fit to point out the obvious. "Without Josie, without a dog, without me, you shall be all alone in this house, Miss Tiggs. Does that… concern you?"

Again she looked at me; those hard little eyes of hers – like raisins – so screwed up I could barely see them. She had finished her ale I noticed, her thick tongue darting out to lick the last remnants of it from her lips. "Alone?" she replied. "Alone!"

How the bulk of her body shook as she bellowed with laughter.

Chapter Five

LONDON fulfilled every expectation.

Father returned a few days after my strange conversation with Miss Tiggs, and announced that we were to leave the following morning. He then locked himself in his study, leaving me free to pack the few belongings that I might require. I was to be away for two nights apparently and we were to occupy rooms in Arthur's townhouse.

Immediately I went in search of Josie, whose help I wanted with the packing, running down the corridors, as I was wont to do, but this time for the best of reasons – the most exciting. She was nowhere to be seen on the ground floor and so I changed direction, heading towards the staircase and taking the steps two at a time in order to begin my search of the bedrooms. Because the majority of rooms lay empty at Mears House did not mean that they could forego cleaning. Dust is a perennial problem here, it gathers and it collects; it covers the bedsteads, the cupboards and the wardrobes, cloaking every last hint of colour.

"Josie! Josie!" I called. "Where are you?"

At last I located her, for she was, as I suspected, in one of the bedrooms, a feather duster in hand. She turned as I burst into the room, no look of startled surprise on her face; rather it appeared as if she was expecting me. What a contrast she was to previous maids, who would quake with fear on realising they had not answered a first call. I am not a tyrant, you understand, but servants are *supposed* to be at your beck and call; one should not be required to go in search of them.

"Ah, there you are," I admonished. "I have been looking all over."

She simply smiled at me.

"I am to go to London!" My next words exploded from me such was my excitement, my *disbelief* that such a thing could finally be happening.

"London, miss?"

"Yes, indeed. I am to be bought new clothing, meet new people."

"What kind of people, miss?"

I stumbled at this – what a strange question!

"Erm… well… Father's friends I should imagine; society people. One of Father's friends has a daughter. Her name is Constance. I shall be meeting with her."

"London," she said again, but her amusement had faded, instead she looked perplexed. Or was that sorrow on her face? It was hard to tell.

I drew closer. "Josie? Are you quite well?"

"I'll miss you."

Her declaration both surprised and touched me. Had I ever been missed by anyone before? Not that I could remember. "I doubt I shall be gone long." And then I remembered that I had wanted to take her too. "I could ask Father if he would permit you to accompany me. It is only fitting that a lady should travel with her maid."

At this, one hand flew to her chest. "Me, travel to London? What a notion!"

What a notion… Those were the words I had thought

when she had offered to walk with me in the grounds of Mears House. That she should be using them in reference to accompanying me to London, at my behest, seemed an irony.

As I stood there, attempting to understand that she had just turned me down, if not yet the reason for it, she smiled again, but this time it failed to reach her eyes.

"I can't go, miss," she muttered at last. "I… There's so much work to be done here."

Work that could not wait? Indeed, who was there to notice if it was left undone? But for some reason I did not want to argue, not with Josie, not today. When I think back, perhaps the reason I declined to press the matter further with either her or Father was simply that I wanted her to miss me; perhaps I *craved* the novelty that someone should. All I could do was nod my head in agreement.

"But you shall help me pack, surely?"

Yes, she would do that.

And so it came to be that I left Mears House in a horse and carriage, accompanied only by my father, with my suitcase stowed beneath the seat.

The journey was an arduous one – Father alternating his gaze between the passing countryside and me, but never saying a word. Often I declined to meet his eyes, but instead focused on the grass-covered hills that were still wet with morning dew and an abundance of trees, some evergreen, some bearing no leaves at all. There was such a strange mixture of emotions in my chest that day – a tight ball that I had to strive to keep from unravelling lest they swamp me. Strangely, I began to miss Mears House. It was my entire world, all I had ever known.

When at last the countryside gave way to villages and

towns I was further astounded. There were houses! So many of them! Not standing alone as Mears House stood alone but side by side or a few feet apart, and so much smaller. In them there would be mothers, fathers, daughters and sons. What would it be like to live in such a way; to be part of something; a family? I could only wonder. The closer we drew to London, the more congested the area became. But it was not only my eyes that were filled with so much new to behold; my nostrils began to flare too, from the smell. Where I lived the air was clean, it was pure – outside at least; it filled your lungs; it rejuvenated you. Here, I feared my lungs might collapse should I inhale too deeply. It was the odour of so many people gathered close together – an animal stench.

About my neck I had a scarf and so I arranged it higher to mask my nose as I leant further forward.

I had imagined the ladies and gentlemen that paraded these streets so often, and the sophistication that being city dwellers – and therefore so much more a part of the modern world – lent them. But it was not only such characters that greeted me. Here was also a lower class of person; the street urchins Mr Dickens was so fond of portraying, scampering this way and that, with clothes that, contrary to what Father had said, made mine appear to be the height of luxury. Businessmen were also in evidence, suited and booted; but rather than grand they seemed weary, as with heads down, they too hurried along. There were women in skirts and aprons, some as gaunt as Josie, others more rotund and rosy-cheeked. They were walking at a more leisurely pace or standing at the street side, selling wares from their baskets –fruit and vegetables, and matches too, boxes and boxes of them. People were gathering around them, poking and prodding at the merchandise, bartering I think it is called, striving to obtain the best price possible. Aside from street vendors, there were shops, a huge variety of them – butchers, bakers and haberdashers, some with their doors open, inviting you in; others that you could enter by appointment only. And there were buses – marvellous things – not pulled along by horses, not all of them, but able to propel themselves, the people inside either sitting or clinging to overhead straps and looking entirely at ease with this mode of transport.

Exciting, repellent, frightening, and enticing – London was all of these to me, and more. It was bursting with life, with the cries and banter of these townsfolk, and part of me wanted to hurl myself from the carriage into the thick of it; ride on one of the buses – although whether that would befit someone of my station I had no clue. The other part wished to return to the comfort and security of Mears House. *Comfort? Security?* That it should suddenly seem to offer both those things was another irony.

I was about to turn towards Father, to ask him *where* in this vast metropolis we were heading, when a figure caught my eye. It was a little boy, a beautiful child with dark hair and eyes and pale skin.

We had come to a temporary halt – the driver cursing whatever obstruction lay in his path and my father practically hanging out of the opposite window to also learn the cause of our delay. There was most definitely a commotion going on, some rowdiness, but my main focus was on this boy, who was standing as still as a statue.

"What the deuce is happening? We shall be late!"

"A street fight, I think, sir. The police are trying to break it up."

"Can you not go around it, for pity's sake?"

"No, sir. Shouldn't be long, sir."

Although I could hear my father and the driver, their voices were muffled, as if distant. The world around this boy seemed to fade too, becoming little more than a series of grey images. Why should he be capturing my attention so, this boy who was standing rigid without uttering a word? His eyes, though, those glorious eyes! He appeared to be about ten years of age, although of course I was no expert at assessing ages. Did his expression hold wonder? I was certain that mine did.

What's your name?

I mouthed the words, feeling suddenly – inexplicably – quite desperate to know.

Eventually, his lips moved to form a smile.

I smiled too. *Hello,* I mouthed again.

He lifted one hand, slowly, tentatively.

I repeated his action, my smile becoming something of a grin. As young as he was, he seemed experienced, as if his life had spanned a thousand years or more.

Your name?

Harry.

As if I had been struck by lightning, I sat back in my seat.

No, he had not opened his mouth. He had not said a word, but still I knew it to be truth. His name was Harry. There it was. There was no doubting the matter.

Father could not have missed my reaction. He stopped berating the driver and resumed alternating his gaze between what lay outside the carriage and myself. Much given to frowning as his usual expression, his countenance was dark, confused, odd to think it, but it was excited too.

Those narrow eyes of his – so different to the boy's – glittered.

Because I had shrunk back; because it took me some moments to summon the courage to look outside again, and only when Father was occupied with doing the same, Harry had in that time disappeared, presumably running through the streets from whence he came.

The carriage began to move, the moment of suspension over.

"We are on our way," I said, feeling the need to say something, even if it was to declare the obvious.

Father settled back into his seat, but his breathing was slightly heavier. As for enquiring of him our destination in London, I thought the better of it. I gazed instead at my hands, clasped together in my lap, and held my tongue.

The miles fell away. I was desperate to look outside once again; to take in the grandeur and the absolute headiness of it all, but I also found myself strangely reluctant – Harry had left quite an impression on me. There was something so very different about him, a little sad too, in spite of his smile. How could it be that one so young could have lived a life beyond his years?

Finally the driver came to a halt. Now the streets were largely empty of people, and instead of shops and vendors, there were houses five stories high, their masonry white; their doors black. No land separated them, but rather they joined shoulder to shoulder, to form a graceful curve.

"We have arrived," Father announced.

"This is Arthur's address?"

"It is."

"This is Hammersmith?"

"Yes," he said, clearly surprised. "How did you know?"

"I saw a sign," I lied.

"Did you, now?" His voice was low, thoughtful. "Did you indeed?"

The driver held the carriage door and extended a hand in order to help me alight. Father followed close behind and together we stood on the pavement outside the house I presumed to be Arthur's, whilst the driver turned his attention towards our luggage. I gazed skywards, marvelling at an abode that was not my own and committing to memory the sight of it so that I could sketch it at a later date, adding to my already copious amounts of drawings. Father had begun striding ahead and I was about to follow obediently when I spied something else – a figure at a window on the second floor, waving at me just as Josie had waved at me, as Harry had also. She appeared to be wearing a white dress, a nightgown perhaps, but most notably her fair hair was flowing free rather than restrained.

I raised my hand yet again to return the gesture, pleasantly surprised at having received the latter two greetings in such a short space of time – how friendly the people in London were turning out to be! Full of hope, I eventually stepped forwards and that is when I noticed Father. Once again he had caught me, his narrow eyes as wide as they could possibly be. He said not a word as he continued to hold me in his sight, but as with Harry, I could read his mind well enough.

What do you see?

Chapter Six

"OH, look at you! You are adorable! Father, I shall take Rosamund to the drawing room immediately so that we can get to know each other better."

It had been something of a whirlwind since we had entered the townhouse, the door having been opened to us by a tall man in uniform – a butler, I believe – Arthur had come into the hall to greet us, shaking my father's hand whilst eyeing me closely, then another person had come flying down the stairs – Constance.

Reaching me, she thrust her hands outwards, grabbing at my arms as she studied me, much like her father had studied me and like my own father tended to do. I felt like a specimen in a jar, unnerved by the attention, but also intrigued as to what they found so interesting about someone so inexperienced and drab in comparison to themselves. However, I was guilty of studying them too. This girl that had hold of me was not wearing a white dress, nor did she have fair hair. Whoever had been waving at me at the window, it could not have been her. Constance was a beauty – Constance Athena Lawton to name her in full, such a grand name compared to plain old Rosamund. From the moment I had laid eyes on her, I was in awe. She was not much older than me, a year or two perhaps, and she had hair that was almost raven in colour, creamy skin and the bluest of eyes – Irish colouring she later told me, courtesy of her mother, who was given to illness apparently and spent her days in bed, being tended. Not that Constance seemed at all disturbed or upset by her mother's poor health, she was another like Josie, seemingly content with what she had; with the world around her. Unlike Josie, however, she had a streak in her that was wild, but wild in a way I envied. She was akin to an exotic creature and yet however fascinated I was by her, she was in turn fascinated by me!

Father and Arthur retired, to where I had no clue, but our destination was the drawing room, located at the front of the house and as grand a room as I had ever seen. It was simply vast, and contained within it so much furniture: two sofas, chairs, rugs, tables, a sideboard and a pianoforte upon which stood a golden candelabrum. There were trinkets on every surface – Constance's mother had a penchant for cherubs apparently – and every wall displayed several paintings. There were portraits, of ancestors perhaps, though none of Constance, and landscapes, two of which were much darker than the others, the figures in them barely distinguishable. As I passed by to sit beside Constance on one of the sofas, a sumptuous affair covered in red velvet, I peered closer. The figures in the paintings were somehow entwined with one another; their limbs flailing; their mouths twisted, some with pleasure, others with something that I would liken more to horror. Quickly I turned my head away, having to swallow hard. They were gruesome pictures, so out of place amongst the other, more commonplace ones. How could one possibly want to sit and admire them?

"So," Constance declared, "tell me about yourself. I

want to know everything!"

Again I was stunned. What could I tell? Nothing interesting, that was for certain. "I… well… I live in the countryside, in Sussex, just Father and I, plus our housekeeper and a maid. My mother… my mother is dead—"

"Dead? Oh, I am sorry!"

"Thank you," I replied. What else could I say? "The house in which we live is Mears House and…" already I had begun to falter. "I enjoy reading and sketching."

"Do you go to school?"

"I have a governess… Had," I corrected myself. "Do *you* go to school?"

She laughed as if the question amused her. "I used to, of course. A boarding school here in London, but no longer." She straightened her back in a proud gesture. "I am too old for school. I am now a lady, ready to tackle society."

Tackle society? What an unusual way to put it!

"Do you… do you have a suitor?" As soon as the words left my mouth I regretted them. How could I be so bold as to ask such a question?

"A suitor?" There passed a few moments in which I silently berated myself, and then Constance burst again into laughter. "I have several suitors, dear Rosamund, all vying for my hand. Sadly, none of them *do* suit me, so I'm afraid I shall have to disappoint them." Dramatically, she clasped her hands to her chest. "I believe in true love and until I find it I shall refuse to marry."

I leant forward, relieved and surprised that she had answered me so readily but also desperate to know more. "And what does your Father have to say about it?"

"He says that in great families there are great sacrifices,

that life does not revolve around love. But, Rosamund," she leaned forward too, "it does, it actually does."

"But your Father…?"

"You must not worry about him," still she was laughing. "He roars like a lion but underneath is as soft as a kitten. He wants me to be happy, I know it."

"And your mother?"

Only slightly did her eyes darken at the mention of her mother. "Mother is given to illness not opinions."

"And you mean to be different?"

"Oh, I do, Rosamund. I do."

I had not realised that Constance had rung for tea, but clearly she had as there was a knock on the door and a maid entered. Not the girl I had seen at the window, she also had dark hair, although there was evidence of white in it. Although not an old, old woman, she was bird-like, her back stooped and her hands quite wizened.

When she had poured the tea and left, I turned to my new friend – for that is what I truly felt she was. A friend. One with whom I had shared confidences.

And so I shared another.

"On arriving here, I saw a girl at one of the bedroom windows. At first I thought it might be you, but then discovered you have dark hair, whereas this girl was fair and was waving to me. I wondered who she might be."

"A girl with fair hair?" Constance checked, her dainty little nose wrinkling.

"Yes."

"How old?"

"Young, quite young, about your age, I would say."

"And she was waving at you?"

"Yes, and she was dressed in white."

She did not respond straightaway, but when she did, her words were curious.

"Why," she said. "It appears you're quite different too."

* * *

My next few hours, indeed my next two days at the Lawton's townhouse, passed in the blink of an eye. Constance was quite giddy with being charged with the task of outfitting me, declaring that we were going to have 'the time of our lives.'

At our disposal was her family's driver and in their horse and carriage we ventured deep into the streets of London, leaving our fathers busy in whatever activities it was that engaged them, certainly, I presumed, nothing as frivolous as tailoring.

Frivolous? No, it was arduous! I was trussed up like a doll at times; my waist pinched with corsets that stole my breath away, dress after dress being buttoned up, whilst my feet were stuffed into boots that also pinched. Constance adored this rigmarole, it was plain to see she was well used to it, but it was making my head spin, so much so I had to beg for mercy; ask that we take a break, perhaps visit a tearoom, which secretly I had been longing to do, having read about such pastimes. Although immersed in my transformation, she finally acquiesced and took me to one of her favourite haunts apparently; a hotel in London's West End called The Gaiety.

As we made our way there, arm in arm, she informed me that women were most welcome in tearooms nowadays. "Society is becoming more enlightened," she insisted, happily chattering in my ear. "As it should." Her voice lowered an octave or two. "Rosamund, people are evolving. This is a good time to be alive."

Who was I to disagree? I simply nodded my head and smiled back at her, finding her enthusiasm, her sheer zest for life, quite infectious. When we arrived at the doors of The Gaiety – having passed several more buses en route, which, to Constance's amusement, I stopped to stare at every time – I was sure we were going to be turned away, in spite of the fact that I was wearing grander clothes than I ever had before. I had to remind myself that we were two young ladies and, although unaccompanied, we were welcome in such establishments; we would be waited on hand and foot.

Stepping inside was like stepping into a world within a world. There were those who sauntered – the ladies and gentlemen of course – and those in uniform whose gait was more determined as they dashed to and fro, carrying silver platters upon which stood elaborate silverware. Without further ado we were shown to our table by one of the waiting staff, Constance having to guide me all the way as my eyes were not just ahead of me but darting all over. The magnificence of it! So many round tables but all a discreet distance apart; the starched white tablecloths; the sumptuousness of the cakes and sandwiches spread upon them in tiered platters; the chatter and polite laughter that filled such a beautiful room; the room itself with its beautiful tiled floor, the art-adorned walls, the Corinthian columns, towering green ferns and oval windows. But more impressive than all of those things – something I had been aware of but had taken an amount of time to fully comprehend – was the light.

As we were seated, all I could do was stare upwards at a chandelier centred in the middle of the ceiling.

"What is that?" I whispered, my heart honestly feeling fit to burst.

"Oh, Rosamund, Rosamund, just as buses, trams and indeed the trains that run beneath our streets are powered by electricity, so too is that."

I turned to her. "Trains that run beneath our streets?"

"Remember you enquired about a rumbling noise earlier? You said you felt as if the ground was shaking. It was then that I told you about the underground train."

She was quite right, she had; but there had been so much to take in, clearly *too* much. "The light," I said again, preoccupied with that.

"Most of the big hotels in London have electrical light nowadays, some shops also. Father has also mentioned that it will be coming to individual homes too at some point. Can you imagine? It will revolutionise the way in which we live."

As she spoke I continued to gaze at the chandelier. The light… it was more beautiful than anything I had ever seen; warm and inviting; pure, with the ability to obliterate all shadows. I wished to reach up and touch it; somehow capture it in my hands as well as my heart. It was magic of the most wonderful kind and I was truly awestruck.

"Rosamund…?"

I shook myself out of the trance I had fallen into. "I am sorry, Constance, so sorry."

Again she laughed, such a wonderful sound, like the tinkling of bells. "I cannot scold you for being so enraptured, I was at first too, but…" She shrugged. "Living here, one really does become used to such things. Indeed, should one happen to grace an establishment that relies on the old ways, one can become quite aggrieved!"

Filled with gratitude suddenly, I reached across the table to take her hand in mine. "Thank you, for bringing me here; for being my friend."

"Of course I am your friend. And I shall insist we spend more time together in the future." Gently retrieving her hand, she raised it to her chest, just above her beating heart. "Oh," she breathed. "Here he is."

I turned my head to discover who she could possibly mean. There was a waiter coming towards us; a young man in a black waistcoat, white shirt and black trousers, with a long white apron tucked into his waistband. Was it this man to which she referred?

I panicked – how was one supposed to order in such a place?

Before I could raise any concerns with Constance, the waiter had come to a halt by the side of our table. He was dashing I supposed, with his hair greased back and blue eyes that were rather piercing, but I thought no more of him than that – he was a waiter. *Just a waiter.* But if I was guilty of such lofty thoughts, it seemed Constance was not. To her, he appeared to be something more, her eyes able to compete with, if not outshine, the electrical light.

"May I take your order, ma'am?" It was a formal enough request from the waiter, were it not for the curve of his mouth.

"Of course…" Constance replied, playfulness in her too. "James, is it?"

"It is, ma'am."

My head swung from side to side witnessing this curious exchange. Did they know each other and not just in this setting?

"We shall have high tea," Constance continued, taking it upon herself to order for us both. "Darjeeling, if you please."

Not only did James' smile widen, he winked at Constance. I may be naïve in the ways of society, but surely a waiter would not dare to wink at his customer?

"Very good, ma'am." He took a step backwards and I thought he was going to turn and leave us, but he was not quite done. His voice low, so as only the two of us could hear amid the general chatter, he added, "I have something else for you, Lady Constance; would it be agreeable to bring that to you, too?"

As my mouth fell open, Constance could only purr. "A gift you mean?"

"Of sorts."

"Oh, the intrigue," she teased. "I shall leave instructions as to when and where."

When he had left us alone, I turned to Constance, my eyes begging for an answer.

"As I have told you, Rosamund," was her sole reply, "it's a good time to be alive."

Chapter Seven

I loathed the thought of returning to Mears House, but return I must. I sat in the carriage with Father, whom I had barely seen these past two days, dressed not in the clothes in which I had arrived, but in white linen and bows. This was not the only change about me, however. I had seen things; I had heard things. Through my encounter with Constance I had been immersed, if only for a short while, in an alternative reality far removed from that to which I was accustomed. Constance and James: I was still amazed by their tryst and how daring she was; how different to anything I had expected.

Of course I insisted that she told me all about it when we were out of earshot.

"We are in love," she had declared.

"You and the waiter?"

"James, his name is James and he is from suitable stock; not the elite, no, I shall grant you that, but a decent family nonetheless." As I stared at her open-mouthed, she continued. "Money cannot make you a good person, Rosamund. It does not make one noble. And some of these families," she gestured about her, although we were alone in our carriage, returning to the townhouse, "who parade themselves, who assume station above others; who imagine themselves to be so high and mighty, they have no money. Do you realise that? It's all theatre. Scratch beneath the surface and you shall find some will not have as much spare change in their pocket as James has. James is very much into politics, into a wide range of subjects; he is so clever, so... informed. So much so that he inspires me. Society is changing, Rosamund. The world is changing. The old ways are disappearing and rather than be afraid, we must embrace it." She had hugged herself at this point; had closed her eyes. "Embrace everything, for everything is new and fascinating."

It was hard not to believe her; I *wanted* to believe her; experience it alongside her. But something did not sit right with me.

"Your Father has no idea about you and James, has he?"

"Of course not." She found the idea that he might, amusing rather than terrifying.

"If he discovers—"

"But I have told you, Rosamund, I can manipulate Father. You must not worry."

That also amazed me. If Father knew I was fraternising with someone from a lower class, I could just imagine the consequences that would befall me. Not that I would do such a thing. Not because I was concerned about anybody's station in life, not after what Constance had said. I felt she was right; people did put on such airs and graces. It was simply because I could not picture myself fraternising with anyone. Besides, her observation applied very much to me too. As refined as I might look thanks to my transformation at her hands, I was on my way back home and home was a place I should be ashamed to invite Constance. Not for her the dusty surfaces of Mears House – the sheer isolation of it, the terrible neglect. When I got home, I would change back into my own clothes and no doubt slip back into my old way of life too. A thought that was now hard to bear.

"Father, when shall we return to London?"

Surely such an investment in my clothing could not be for one occasion? Also I had really only been seen by Constance, not by 'society' as such. As I have mentioned, I barely saw Father and Arthur; I had listened out for them but I never overheard the low whisper of conversation travelling towards me from another room. Where had they gone during the time I was there? What had they been doing?

Father was reading some papers, handwritten notes, with not just words upon them but drawings too, or rather symbols.

"Father," I dared to prompt.

"Soon, Rosamund, soon," he answered; not bothering to glance up he was so engrossed in what he held.

I should have loved more detail, but I was no Constance; I would not press further. What I had learnt was good enough – at some point I was going back, I would see Constance again, I would hear all about her liaison with James. She was bursting to tell someone and had declared how glad she was to have me in her life; a confidante, a position I felt extraordinarily proud to hold. But as much as I looked forward to our next meeting, I also found myself longing to see Josie too – and found it peculiar that this was the case. In a world far lonelier than London, she had become something of an anchor. She was the only factor that made Mears House seem like home rather than a place in which to exist. Not Father certainly, and as for Miss Tiggs... I sighed, longing again for a dog; a faithful companion – someone to stand by me; to look out for me; to love me. No, I had not the boldness of Constance. I could never ask Father to fulfil my yearning in that respect. But I had Josie, and her smile, as bright as Constance's smile, offered relief as well as a degree of solace.

Despite that, my heart plummeted when we turned onto the path that led to Mears House. It was home. And yet I felt home*less*, as if I did not belong anywhere. *Like Harry.*

Harry? How odd that he should spring to mind – the urchin boy. But it seemed the correct comparison to make – Harry had appeared homeless too. I recalled all those I had seen on the streets of London; the colourful and the less colourful, those who were decidedly more grey, who had stared at me as I passed them by; whose faces had expressed so many emotions – bewilderment even, on occasions. Constance had seemed oblivious to them, but then Constance had her mind on other matters!

It was Miss Tiggs that opened the door to us, her rotund figure such a contrast to the Lawtons' butler, and, although she deferred to my Father, who swept past her and on towards his study, those notes still clutched in his hand, she all but sneered at me. Immediately my hackles rose. Such disdain! Such disrespect! I should have liked to take a piece of her sour cheese and shove it down her throat, a thought that amused me – the sheer wickedness of it – Constance and her wild ways had clearly had more of an influence than I had bargained for.

But where was Josie?

Leaving my suitcase at the foot of the stairs, I called out for her. Father had not yet reached his study but he turned and looked at me, a scowl on his face. I expected him to reprimand me, perhaps for being so loud, but he shook his head, narrowed those eyes and entered his study at last, slamming the door behind him.

Yet again, Josie was nowhere to be found on the ground floor, and so I made my way upstairs. To my surprise, I found her in the corridor that led to the attic.

"I have been calling for you." I deliberately refrained from saying 'again'. "Have you…" I could feel a frown developing, however, "…been into the attic?"

It was not my imagination; her green eyes lit up on seeing me, but their expression was also guarded as if she was suddenly wary. "The attic, miss? No, why ever would I?"

"Then why are you in this corridor?"

"I'm dusting."

Sure enough, in her hand was the feather duster – an almost permanent feature.

She stretched her hand upwards and waved the duster around. "See? There are cobwebs everywhere." When still I did not say a further word, she added, "It's my job, miss, to keep everything clean."

"But you have not been into the attic?" Why I felt the need to check this again was beyond me.

"No need. It's clean enough in there."

"Josie—"

"Your suitcase, where is it?"

"I left it at the foot of the stairs."

"I should fetch it?"

"Yes. Thank you."

"I'll bring it to your bedroom."

"Thank you," I said again as she squeezed past me.

Before I turned to follow her, I stared at the attic door, a longing deep within me to go inside; to hide suddenly – but from what? The urge was so strong that I actually took several steps towards the door, my hand reaching out to touch the handle; to turn it; twist it. A haven. It still represented that to me and was perhaps the only room, apart from the library, that made this house bearable. But clean inside? What could Josie possibly mean by that? It was cluttered; it was dust-ridden.

Clean.

I continued to ponder as I turned and made my way back to my bedroom.

* * *

Life resumed at Mears House. Father returned to London on his own and when he came back, he barely called for me; barely had anything to do with me in fact. He would eat and drink in his study; might even have slept in there, who knew? His bedroom was quite a distance from mine and I had no reason to keep a constant watch on it. I could hear him well enough on occasion, though. There would come a crash, and then a series of curses as he careered down corridors and into the walls and furniture; whatever alcohol he had poured into himself rendering it impossible to walk in a straight line.

Father's drinking was getting worse. Was he unhappy? Agitated? Did he regret the money spent on bedecking me? Would Miss Tiggs leave if he could no longer pay her wage; would Josie? And if so, then what would become of us all?

Such thoughts and more would tumble into my mind, until I fancied I should like a drink too – something to calm my nerves. Father would notice, however, if any of his precious liquor was gone; he would come chasing after me for certain then. And so I did as I always did: filled the endless hours reading and drawing, creating picture after picture – of London and its busy streets; the townhouse; my mother; Constance and her beau James, and… Harry. Often I would draw Harry and those eyes in which I had momentarily drowned. Sometimes, if my legs grew restless, I would leave the sketches in the drawing room, fetch my coat and let myself out for a walk. Soon it would be December, and I wondered if we might have snow. I was always glad to see it, as it dressed everything so prettily, although I was not so glad at night when the rooms became so cold that even my teeth would ache! It was not snowing on this day, however, but damp and grey; a typical winter's day with nothing to relieve the gloom. Once again I thought of the tearoom that Constance and I had visited, with its electric lights. Soon they would light up London in its entirety, so Constance had said. Having begun my walk, I glanced over my shoulder as I hurried towards the woods. Mears House might be quite different if it was lit up. It could be cheerful rather than dour, a vision that would not quite bear fruit.

As I neared the edge of the woods, I shivered. I had returned from London with a new coat, but I was saving it, as I was my new collection of dresses. I was back in my old threadbares and regretted at least not adorning my head with my new hat, and my hands with some velvet gloves. A mist had begun to develop – the 'Sussex Particular' I rather jokingly called it. It was hovering just above the trees as I approached but gradually it descended in a series of wispy tendrils that held me quite enthralled. Continuing to walk, I watched as these tendrils broke from the mass to weave their way in and around so many naked branches, curling like smoke, as a lover might curl his fingers around the wrists of the lady he adored – a possessive gesture, a possessive lover.

My imagination had been ignited – not only because of my books but also due to Constance and James. Was he her lover? Certainly she had hinted as much. Constance who was brave, bold and beautiful – everything I wished to be; who had her father wrapped around her little finger: if only I could do that with *my* father.

If only he loved me.

Realising once again that he did not, that *no one* did, I began to feel quite miserable. There existed someone who liked me well enough; Constance, or at least I fancied she did, but there were times when I longed for more than that. Tears had begun to fill my eyes and soon they would spill onto my cheeks. I was not given to self-pity ordinarily, but on occasion what I lacked overwhelmed me. As I was contemplating this, something odd happened. The tendrils of mist changed. If there had been anything enchanting about them before – the fey quality of their wispiness perhaps – there certainly was not now. They had darkened considerably; were blacker than a rain cloud waiting to burst. *Like fingers pointing at me.*

As well as confusion, I felt colder than ever – as if those tendrils were not in the distance but were in fact swooping towards me; piercing my clothes; my flesh; diving into the heart of me to find there a fragile thing that could so easily be crushed.

With numb hands I began to bat at my sleeves. "What is this? What is happening?" So quickly rational thought deserted me. "Leave me alone! Please. Leave me be!"

But I knew I would not be able to halt them in their approach. They would be as slippery as eels.

"Stop!" My voice was a screech. "Keep away!"

Although my feet felt as if they had taken root, I forced myself to turn; to attempt an escape. It was with deep shock I realised how far into the woods I had roamed; to the very edge of it, and therefore escape back to the house seemed an impossible distance to cover.

Rosamund, you must at least try!

Heeding my own instruction, I began to run, but the path ahead was far from clear – it was strewn with tree stumps and branches. My foot snagging on something, I felt myself topple, certain that as I hit the ground the tendrils would have formed a mass all of their own; that they would fall upon me to either devour or suffocate me.

"Help!" I screamed again, but in complete despair. Who was there to help me? Who was there to even believe me? This was nonsense, pure imagination… or madness. Indeed, it might be that.

"Miss! Miss! You're safe. Take my hand."

More bewildered than ever, I looked up. There, in front of me was Josie, her red hair still tucked beneath her cap; a shawl covering her thin shoulders.

"Josie, what—?"

"Come on, miss. Let me help."

I reached up. Her hand, as it took mine, was so small, but it was warm; that registered straight away, and I was entirely glad of it.

Back on my feet, I fixed my eyes ahead, only ahead, refusing to glance behind me. Josie, it seemed, did the same. I offered no explanation as to why I had fallen and she offered none as to why she was so deep in the woods. She simply put her arm around my shoulders and, because of the pain in my knee where I had fallen and struck the ground, I leant against her. Together we limped back to the house.

Chapter Eight

THE cut on my knee was worse than I had realised. Once inside Mears House, we hurried to the drawing room. Ordinarily, I supposed we would have gone to the kitchen. Josie had indeed suggested that, for after all, water would be more readily available there, but I had refused. I had no wish to see Miss Tiggs; to witness a face that could not care less that I had hurt myself, or that I had been so frightened. But Josie cared – her expression made that known. Even when she sat me down on the sofa, she would not let me go, her grip on my shoulders remaining firm.

"All is well, Josie," I tried to assure her, "but if you could bring me some rags, it will help to stem the bleeding. Silly me," I muttered. "I am so clumsy."

"You're no such thing," was her response before she left me at last, returning promptly with not just a collection of rags stuffed into the pocket of her apron but a bowl of fresh water, which she held between her hands, as though it were a sacred chalice. She laid it upon the table, having to push aside my sketches to do so. Again I noticed her glance at them, her hand moving one or two in order to gain a closer view.

"Did you tell Miss Tiggs of my accident?" I enquired as she knelt in front of me, lifted my skirt above my knee and gently removed my stocking. I flinched as she had to peel it where skin and wool had melded, but her hand was steady as she worked diligently away. When it was done, the green of her eyes met the dark of mine.

"What *did* happen, miss?"

"What where you doing in the woods?"

She laughed a little and I did too when I realised how absurd we sounded - meeting each other's question with one of our own. At this rate we would accomplish nothing!

Having bandaged my knee, Josie turned to stoke the fire. Even so, there was still such a chill in my bones. As the flames began roaring I decided to answer her question, although in truth I was not entirely sure where to begin.

"I had simply gone for a walk, just to the woods, where I often go."

Josie nodded her head at my words, rising to stand before me.

"Please," I insisted. "Take a seat."

Obliging, she perched on the chair opposite.

I took a deep breath, still with no clue as to how I should explain what had happened. I winced inwardly, unsure if I *wanted* to remember, and then, quite suddenly, as though my lips were as strong-willed as Constance's, words poured from me.

"There was a mist; I could see it clearly hanging over the trees, and then it was somehow *in* the trees, curling around the branches – little wisps, tendrils, as I thought of them." I shook my head. "Or a lover's hand, but one with cruelty in it, because quickly they began to grasp and snatch; darting here and there as if searching. The more I stared, transfixed, the more defined in shape and substance they became. So many tendrils. They grew darker and darker, not like mist at all now, but something else; something abhorrent. They congealed – that is the only description I have – to form something separate, and I knew… I knew that if I continued to stare at them, if I grew even more frightened, they would turn their focus on me rather than the trees."

I had begun to sob – loud wracking sobs that may have had my father come running had he been home to witness this commotion. Thankfully, only Josie and I were in the house, and Miss Tiggs of course, but she could not hear, being far away in the kitchen. Even if she had, she would ignore me and continue to sit by the fireside, supping her beer and warming her over-inflated body, thinking nothing of it.

"I am sorry, so sorry. I do not understand why I am suddenly overcome."

"There, there, miss."

Josie's sweet words only made me cry more and so she stopped, waiting for the outpouring to run its course. When at last it did, she handed me another rag so that I might blow my nose. I apologised again as I wiped my eyes.

"When you…" Josie hesitated, her eyes downcast for a moment, her teeth gnawing at her lip. She took a deep breath before continuing. "How were you feeling when you saw what you did?" She tapped at her chest. "In here, I mean."

"Well…" I tried to remember. "Scared. Of course I was scared. I have never witnessed such a thing before. And sad, definitely sad."

"Why sad, miss?"

"Because…" Was there shame in admitting it? "I felt that no one loved me… my Father…"

"What else?"

"What else?" I queried. Was this not enough? "I felt... I felt... angry."

"Just angry?"

I shook my head, confused by her intent to probe deeper and deeper. And then I realised, it *was* more than anger that I had been feeling; it was rage, it was bewilderment; it was loneliness and it was terror. They were all there within me, even when I was unable to acknowledge them – when I refused to – bubbling below the surface. Extreme emotions, *negative* emotions; they *characterised* me.

There was realisation on Josie's face also.

"That's why you saw what you did, miss," she said before slowly rising to her feet, touching me lightly on the shoulder and seemingly drifting from the room.

I did not call her back; I did not ask that she elaborate. There was no necessity.

I knew what she meant.

* * *

"Rosamund! Rosamund!"

I awoke to my name being used; a whispered sound, but urgent. I had been deep in sleep and I struggled to lift my head, turning towards the voice.

"Father? Is that you?"

There was indeed a figure sitting on a chair in my bedroom; a hazy outline, almost as black as the room itself. The figure was perfectly still, staring at me.

The sight gave me the impetus required to push myself up into a sitting stance.

"Father?" I said, trying to make sense of what was going

on; to remember the events that had led me here.

I had fallen in the woods, hurt my leg, and then later on, had sat for hours by the fireside, Josie bringing me some food from the kitchen, although I was uninterested in it and had pushed it aside. All this had happened yesterday after… after I had seen something. When she had returned with my food, Josie had sat with me again, her presence such a comfort. We did not talk as we had talked earlier; there was simply no need; we understood each other, she and I, although how that could be, I was quite unsure. But there was a new ease between us and I felt happier to know she lived at Mears House too – the house and I both benefited from her presence.

But this presence – the one who had come into my room; who sat and stared at me; who whispered my name – made the house feel dour again; chilled.

With a speed that was preternatural, the figure rose from the chair and arrived by my side, bending over me; forcing me to lie back down.

Was it a dream? Another nightmare? I had so many nightmares; sometimes they plagued me. Little wonder, I supposed – this lonely house, hidden as it was, was a house that *bred* nightmares.

I could bear it no longer. I closed my eyes, screwed them up tight, wishing I could somehow shut off my other senses too.

Whisky – it has such a sour smell.

That alone confirmed the identity of the figure. When had he returned? Certainly, I had retired to bed later than usual and there had been no sign of him.

How I wished I could scream, for Josie; for some sort of protection. But there was nothing and no one.

"Father?" I tried so hard to disguise the whimper in my voice.

"Like her," he slurred. "You are so like her."

"Who?"

"She taunted me. As do you."

"Father, I am tired. Yesterday I had an accident you see—"

"It shall not happen again."

Despite myself I was curious. "What, Father?"

"I shall make sure of it."

"I am not sure I understand what you mean."

"Arthur says to tread carefully, that you could go the same way. But all is well for Arthur; all is not well for me. Arthur be damned!"

His hand shot out, a blackened thing, to grab me by the shoulder. His grip was tight at first and I flinched, but then it grew looser. This brought only temporary relief, however, as something more alarming began to occur. With his fingers, he stroked the cotton of my nightshift, and his mouth came even closer.

"So like her," he continued to murmur. "So like her."

"Father, please…" I found myself begging yet again. "I really am so very tired. I was trying to tell you that I fell in the woods yesterday and hurt my knee. Josie was very kind, she tended to me, but it is still sore, Father. Father, stop, let me go!"

I slapped his hand away from me and with my legs pushed myself backwards out of the bed, falling to the floor.

"Come here, you little wretch," he called. "You are mine to do with as I wish."

Quickly, I got to my feet, and as I did, Father hurled

himself at me.

I had to defend myself; drink had turned him into a beast, the worst I had ever seen him, and although the darkness cloaked his eyes, I could sense well enough the intent in them. Thankfully, I was close to the fireside. I lunged towards it, snatching up the black iron poker and brandishing it in front of me.

"Stay away! I beg you. Just… stay away."

He came to a halt. "You would dare to strike me?" he questioned, such cruel laughter in his voice.

"You would dare to touch me?" I said, determined that he would not.

Again there was a peel of laughter, but I noticed he did not move further. In truth he could have torn that poker from my hand quite effortlessly.

"Father, the whisky; I think it has taken its toll on you tonight."

"Oh? You are now an expert on such matters, are you?"

"I do not wish to fight. I just want to be left alone to sleep."

"What is it about you, Rosamund? What was it about her?"

His words were such a mystery to me.

"Why do you deny it? WHY?"

As he screamed at me, my legs threatened to buckle.

"You would do better to put that poker down."

If there had been any respite from his approach, it was now over. He was advancing on me again and even with a weapon in hand, I felt defenseless.

Tears began to fall from my eyes as I first held up the poker, and then lowered it. I could not hit out. It was not in me to do so. I knew then I was a victim – *his* victim.

"That is better. Much, much better," his voice had taken on a soothing quality that made my skin crawl. "If you would only do as instructed, Rosamund, all will be well."

His breath, oh his breath! I turned my head to the side as the poker dropped from my hand and crashed to the floor; repulsed by it, by him. In me there was only resignation as I succumbed to whatever my fate should be.

Only resignation, Rosamund?

As his hands grabbed my shoulders again, as he dragged me closer to him, I remembered my conversation with Josie. She was quite right. There was not *only* resignation in me, or fear. She had made me realise this. There existed a whole host of emotions, and of these, my rage at least matched his.

I allowed it to rise upwards; indeed I coaxed it to crawl out of whatever recess it lurked in. I allowed it the freedom to conquer all other emotions; to drown them out entirely. I focused not on Father's hands as they began to paw at me, but on my anger. It was a living thing, I was sure of it; a thing apart. It had such energy!

I heard it first – the rattling.

And then he heard it.

Both our heads turned towards the door.

"Josie?" I breathed.

"Who is that?" Father questioned, becoming stockstill.

Still the rattling continued, reminding me of how it did that on occasions when I was in the attic. I had always presumed it was Father coming to find me, but only daring to venture so far. I was safe in the attic, but not safe here, in my bedroom. This time it was clearly not him, but if it were Josie or Miss Tiggs surely they would call out or announce themselves. Next came a banging – a fierce banging, like so many fists pummelling, pummelling – and the door shuddered in its frame as a consequence. Whoever was responsible would come tearing in soon, surely, having torn it off its hinges. Though alarmed, I was grateful for the sudden commotion and for how it had distracted the man grabbing at me. It had caused him to step away from me, his breathing coming in short sharp gasps, his chest heaving.

"What the devil?" he was saying. "What is it? What have you done, Rosamund?"

What had *I* done? Nothing! I had done absolutely nothing.

As abruptly as the rattling had started, it stopped.

I said not a word, and nor did Father. We stood there for an age; mute.

Eventually he turned towards me, making an attempt with shaking hands to straighten his cravat. "We are to return to London."

"When?" was all I could think to ask.

"We shall leave tomorrow."

Having informed me of this, he left my side and returned to the door, reached for the handle and tentatively opened it. As he did so, I flinched and I am certain he must have done the same, myself half expecting more of those tendrils to come pouring through; to grab me as Father had grabbed me, and this time there would be no escape. When nothing of the sort occurred; when all that met us was the darkness of the landing beyond, his sigh of relief was as audible as mine. Before he disappeared out of sight, however, he stopped, once more a hazy distant figure.

"Arthur be damned," he repeated. "It *is* time."

Chapter Nine

TIRED and bewildered I rose early that morning, retrieving my suitcase from my wardrobe and laying it upon the bed. I had not managed to sleep a wink after Father left, too distressed by all that had occurred. Strangely, much as I was looking forward to seeing Constance and hearing all about any further escapades with James, I was dreading it too. As well as Father's actions, his words had stuck in my mind. *It is time*, he had said. Time for what? There had been such an ominous note to his tone, all slurring and signs of drunkenness suddenly gone. As I watched him leave my room, a thought had crossed my mind – should I run to the attic and hide there? I did not know what kept Father from that room, but something did – something that by contrast, welcomed *me*. He was becoming more and more unpredictable. Last night… I shuddered just as the doorframe had, remembering it. What had possessed him? For that is what he had seemed, a man possessed.

The knock on the door gave me cause to yelp.

At once I reminded myself who it was – Josie, come to assist with my morning ablutions.

"Enter," I called, and the door opened. There she stood, her smile yet again tinged with sorrow.

A part of me longed to rush and throw myself into her

arms; glean some comfort, *any* comfort, and she would oblige – as much a friend to me as Constance – but I desisted. Another part of me wanted no one to touch me ever again.

Her gaze moved from me to the suitcase. "You're going back then, miss?"

"Yes," I replied.

"You're not happy about it?"

"I am. I am just… tired. Josie, was it you that tried my door in the night?"

I knew not why I asked. It was not her. I had previously made my mind up on that.

"No," she said, coming fully into the room. "Was anything amiss?"

My bottom lip trembled. Indeed, everything was amiss, but I held my nerve, lest I disintegrated into a blubbing mess. "I really must pack," I said instead.

We passed the next hour doing exactly that until all my new fine clothing was folded and neatly stowed, all apart from my travelling dress, which Josie helped me into before sitting me at my dressing table and brushing my hair until it shone.

"You've such pretty hair," she murmured, almost to herself as much as me, and the compliment – so genuinely delivered – threatened to produce tears yet again.

I must be strong.

"You must be strong."

Her next words – an exact echo of my thoughts – startled me.

I jerked my head away from the brush as I asked what she had meant.

"In London, be careful," was her steady reply. "I've

heard such tales."

Although I was sitting with my back to her, I could see her face well enough in the mirror, and perhaps it was because the mirror's silver was tarnished, that she looked almost as grey and hazy as Father had looked the previous night. But unlike Father, it was not darkness that surrounded her; she appeared to shine, as though illuminated by London's new electric light. I blinked two or three times before asking what tales she referred to. Had she read such stories as I had myself? If so, I was surprised she could read; or, and this was more probable, had she been told these tales?

"Josie?" I prompted.

Her hands left my hair as she sighed. "It's just there are so many people, and some of them, miss, are not who they seem to be."

"My father is one who is not as he seems," I said, in spite of myself. A gentleman? In the eyes of society perhaps, but never again in my eyes.

"There are plenty like him. Their goal is the same."

I was astounded. Josie was a simple country girl, but sometimes you would not think it. "How can you know all this? Have you been to London before, and if so, why have you not spoken of it until now? Has a member of your family been to London?"

She shook her head, those red wisps of hair flicking from side to side.

"I wish I could go with you, that's all."

"You were aghast when that very thing was suggested before now," I reminded her. "You said you had too much work to do here."

"There's much work to be done everywhere."

At this, I grew impatient with her. "You are talking in riddles!"

"Take care, miss, that's all I meant to say. Be who you are. And..."

"Yes, Josie?"

"Remember what you're capable of."

Again, she was talking nonsense... or was she? Indeed, look at what I had achieved just a few short hours previously; I had saved myself in spite of my terror. I had stood there in defiance against my father with a poker in my hands, for goodness sake! Although in actuality, my salvation had been the banging and crashing at the door. Had that been its purpose, to save me? Or was it more akin to what I had witnessed in the woods and was something that wanted only to devour me? Questions, questions! My head was full with them. "All will be well," I heard myself saying. "Do not fuss so."

Although I registered the hurt on Josie's face, she did as I bade her. I was about to leave this cold, tainted room for the splendour of Constance's family home once again; there I would have another bedroom to myself, one with fine sheets on the bed in contrast to those that had worn thin on the rickety frame of mine. How long this time? More than two nights? I had no idea. Would I ever come back to Mears House? I shook my head to rid it of such thoughts. Of course I would. I had to.

Tired of thinking, tired of talking too, I had to go downstairs to the hall in order to be ready the moment that Father wanted to leave.

"If you will bring my case, Josie..."

"Yes, miss. Of course, miss."

I had almost reached the door when Josie caught up

with me. My suitcase, however, was not in her hands. Something else was.

"I found it," she offered by way of explanation.

"Where?" I asked, taking the object from her, feeling compelled to. It was a necklace, its green coloured stones resplendent on a fine golden chain. Immediately, I clasped it to my breast, feeling a faint vibration from it, a slight pulsing that instead of causing alarm, only brought comfort. "Where did you find it?" I asked again.

"I was dusting in one of the bedrooms, the smallest one. There was a vase and I knocked it over; it was an accident of course. This was in it."

I did not want to give it back. I wanted to place it around my neck, but if Father saw it, he would ask a dozen questions about it, no doubt. Furthermore, he might rip it from me and trade it – for this was no common trinket; it looked expensive.

"Keep it about you," Josie said, reading my mind for the second time, "but hidden, perhaps in a purse or something." She paused. "Think of it as a…" it seemed she had to search for the right word "… a talisman, that's it."

"A talisman?" I repeated, only half amused. "It shall protect me?"

"It will." In contrast to me, she remained solemn. "Help comes in many different forms."

She was once again implying that I would need help. I let this go, aware that time was racing by and that Father must not be kept waiting. Obeying her instruction, I secreted the necklace in my purse. In the hall, Father was indeed pacing to and fro. He looked wretched, his eyes bloodshot, tremors coursing through him still.

"Come on," he said, avoiding all eye contact.

Miss Tiggs was at the door. She dropped her usual ungainly curtsey to Father as he passed her, but simply glared at me. No matter. I clutched my purse in my hands, my fingers cupping those stones, feeling the warmth of them penetrate both material and skin, continuing upwards towards my torso, banishing any chill that lingered.

I climbed into the carriage and took my seat opposite Father. He took some notes from a leather case beside him and began reading, once more refusing to look at me or indeed speak to me, this lasting the entire journey. I did not care; I welcomed it. I sought no explanation from him. There was nothing he could say that *would* explain.

We were just a few miles from the Lawton household and I was gazing out of the window, half wondering if I should see Harry, that beautiful little urchin boy, when realisation suddenly struck me; the necklace – I had seen it before. It had been draped across a high-collared dress in a photograph that was hidden. It was the very same! I could see it in my mind's eye as clear as a summer's day.

Surreptitiously, I reached into my purse, as if to retrieve a handkerchief, once again touching the stones but briefly this time, not wishing to alert Father; to have him challenge me on what I might be doing. Oh, the thrill of them; the sense of wellbeing I acquired from them – the *protection*.

Clumsy Josie. Clever Josie. She had found Mother's necklace.

Which now raised another question: What had Mother needed protection from?

Or rather whom?

* * *

This time, when we arrived at the townhouse, there was no mysterious figure at the window waving, and no Constance either, flying down the stairs ready to embrace me. Had she not known I was coming? If she had, I felt certain she would be here.

As the butler ushered us into the hallway, and the maid – the one with the wizened hands – who had brought us tea directed me upstairs towards my bedroom, leaving Father to seek out Arthur, I kept alert for any sign of Constance.

My bedroom at the townhouse was on the first floor and Constance's on the third, not that I had paid a visit to it; I had not, but she had imparted this information on the previous occasion that we had visited. When the maid had finished unpacking my suitcase – so slowly it seemed, fussing and tutting to herself, about what I could not tell you – and left me alone at last, I hurriedly retrieved the necklace. What were these stones, I wondered, which were as green as Josie's eyes? Constance would know. She knew everything.

And so I resolved to find her. Leaving my room, checking that the passage was clear, I returned to the staircase and ascended quietly past the second floor and up to the third where the stairs carried onwards to the servant quarters above.

There were several rooms on this floor, and all doors were closed. Which one was Constance's room? Taking a deep breath; remembering no harm could befall me whilst I had the necklace about my person, I knocked timidly on the first door and called Constance's name. There was no reply. This happened a second and a third time, but at the fourth door I heard movement inside, if not an acknowledgement.

Filled with hope, I gently pushed the door open.

"It is I," I whispered. "Rosamund."

Because the curtains were closed it was dark, but what characterised this room was the smell – sweet and sickly, it made me screw my eyes shut temporarily as an urge to retch came upon me. Quickly, I reprimanded myself. *Think of your friend, Rosamund, not yourself, clearly she is ill.* Stepping further into the room, I noticed movement on the bed. There was someone lying beneath a thick coverlet. There was a fire roaring too, which only served to intensify the awful stench.

"Nell, is that you?"

Nell?

The voice that had asked was low and croaky. If this was Constance, she must be feeling wretched.

If?

Panic seized me. What if it were not? Constance's mother was much given to illness apparently, spending much of her time in her room. What if her bedroom was also on the third floor? How foolish I had been to go exploring. Why had I behaved so recklessly? I should have waited patiently for Constance to come and find me.

In an attempt to rectify my terrible mistake, I began to back from the room, but I was too late. The figure was now squirming on the bed, craning its neck to see me.

"Nell, is it you? Have you got it?"

"I… I am not Nell," I stammered.

I could see the rudiments of a face but nothing further, the darkness obscuring my vision.

"But have you got it?" The person – a woman, Constance's mother, it had to be – asked again.

"Got what?"

"Did she send you?"

"Nell?"

"Tell me whether you have it!" This time her voice was much higher, and filled with a desperation that made me feel quite desperate too.

"I am sorry," I said, still intent on retreating, my hand on the door ready to close it behind me; to end this escapade.

"Do not go!" the woman commanded. "Come closer."

Although I was desperate to flee, I could not. If she was indeed Constance's mother, she was the Lady of this house and therefore to be obeyed.

As I began to tentatively make my way closer, the door swung shut behind me and I jumped upon hearing it. Nonetheless I continued towards the bed, my only solace knowing that I had my talisman with me. That Josie had even called it so was comfort enough. To know that Mother had owned it, more comfort still.

The woman shuffled and groaned, pushing herself semi-upright.

I noticed a jug of water on the table. "Would you like some?" I said, pointing to it.

The laughter she emitted was harsh. "No. That is not what I want. Who are you?"

"I am Rosamund. I am here with my father, my father being a friend of Mr Lawton's."

"My husband?" she repeated, shuddering, I was certain of it. "What is your father's business with him?"

Before I could answer she was seized by a violent coughing fit, one hand flailing towards me as she managed to utter in between, "My handkerchief, fetch it."

Next to the jug of water was a handkerchief, such a delicate thing, made of lace and so at odds for the purpose for which it was about to be used. When I offered it to her, she grabbed it, our fingers briefly touching and as they did, a series of images flashed through my mind, each and every one of them tortured. It lasted moments, mere moments, but what I saw scarred me. A woman, so like Constance and certainly as beautiful, as exuberant, as full of life and energy, quickly becoming a wretched, weakened thing; a mere shadow of her former self. But why? Because she was terrified, that was why.

"Madam…" I uttered, wanting now only to embrace this stinking, sweating creature before me who was filling such a delicate handkerchief with blood – for the visions had prompted such an extent of sympathy. Instead I watched as she threw the handkerchief aside; as she beckoned for the water she had only recently refused.

After taking a few laboured sips, she sank back against her pillow.

"I need it you see," she said. "This cough…"

"Are you referring to your medicine?" I asked, wondering where it was and whether I could administer that too.

"It… It helps… With everything."

"Where is it?" I looked about me, searching for a bottle of some sort.

"Need more… Nell… but he, he controls it… controls me."

He? Who did she mean?

"Mr Lawton?" I queried.

She nodded, a brief gesture. "Mad," she said. "Worse… Evil."

"Evil?" My eyes felt as if they would burst from my

head. Was she implying Arthur was evil?

"Shall I… open the curtains?" I was desperate to have some light in this room, an open window too, to let some of the stench out. I was sure that if I continued breathing it in I would become as sick as her.

When she did not answer, I took it upon myself to prise the curtains apart, but as I made my way towards them, she cried out 'NO!' My blood curdled to hear such a terrible sound. I swung round to look at her, half in fear, half in surprise.

"It hurts, damn you!" Spittle flew from her mouth. "The light hurts."

Sobbing now, she appeared to collapse in on herself.

I continued to stand there, frozen with indecision. What was I to do? Go to her or call someone?

"Madam…" How like Josie I sounded. "If you will tell me where to find Nell… Or Constance, I can fetch Constance."

"Constance is lost."

"Lost?" I shook my head. "If she is not at home, then perhaps she is out, taking tea?"

"She is lost," again she insisted. "*I* am lost."

I had been uneasy until now, but when Constance's mother began keening and to rock to and fro, I was horrified. If someone should hear her – Nell, or worse, Arthur – and found me here, upsetting her, I would be in trouble beyond imagining.

"Madam, please, I apologise for coming here, I should not have done so."

I reached out to her again, meaning only to offer comfort, but, as had previously happened, the moment our hands touched, visions filled my mind. I had no power to stop them or withdraw my hands for she had brought hers over mine, both now clutching at me as desperately as if she were drowning and I her only saviour.

Rather than look into her reddened eyes, I shut my own and the images became even clearer. A young woman waiting anxiously at the window for her beau to appear and gasping with delight when she saw him; such a dapper young gentleman, clad head to toe in finery. It was this house he was visiting – not Arthur's then, as I had presumed, but belonging to this woman in the bed in front of me. A charmer, yes, he was certainly that, and handsome too in a slightly austere way. This girl, this woman – Helena was her name – was very much in love with Arthur. Another image: an argument, not between Helena and Arthur but between Helena and an older woman. Her mother? A wedding, such a joyful occasion ordinarily, but there was sadness on Helena's face and no mother in attendance. There were hardly any people at all. This house again, Arthur now the master of it. What had happened to Helena's mother? Or to her father, of whom I have seen no sign? Now she is alone in her bedroom, holding a picture of her mother in her hands as I have done so often myself. She is weeping, and she is confused. *The accident, Mother, the fall... were you pushed? Did Arthur push you?* One hand falls to her belly, her rounded belly – she is with child. A daughter will soon be born – Constance. Helena despairs. *Trapped. Both of us are trapped, in my house, MY house, not his. Do not be fooled, little one. Do not be taken in as I was.*

Having seen more than I could bear, I snatched my hand back, the sheer force of my action taking us both by surprise.

The woman – Helena – was staring at me.

"Who are you?" she croaked at last. "*What* are you?"

"I have told you that my name is Rosamund. I am your daughter's friend, nothing more. I… I need to continue looking for her."

This time I did back away. Resolutely. Nothing she could say, no command she could issue, would stop me. I reached the door, grabbed the handle and yanked at it.

"I must find her," I said again, an attempt at least to explain my swift departure.

"And I have told you," she returned, just as I closed the door, "Constance is lost."

Chapter Ten

"CONSTANCE! Thank the Lord! There you are."

Having fled from Helena Lawton's room, reeling from what had transpired there and how my imagination had run amok, filling my head with such nonsense about a woman of whom I knew nothing, I had dashed the length of the corridor, descended several flights of steps, and somehow found my way back to my room, praying all the while that I would not meet a soul en route, not even my friend.

Safe in my bedroom, I began to pace up and down, feeling both terrified and mystified. Finally, I sank onto my bed and fell into a deep and mercifully dreamless sleep, my fevered brain as much in need of respite as my body. When I awoke it was to find not the pitch black of night but the bright sunlight of morning. Nearby sat a person – not Father this time, and again I was extremely grateful. It was Constance.

Rubbing at my eyes, marvelling that I had slept for so long, I sat up, my arms immediately reaching out for her. Readily she entered my embrace.

She smelt so sweet, so clean, such a contrast to her mother.

"You are not lost, as I had feared," I murmured. "You are not lost."

Clearly confused by my words, she pulled away slightly.

"Why should I be lost?" she asked, her eyes even brighter than before; her skin so flawless – she was perfect, this girl in front of me. To think of any harm coming to her...

Panic set in, though I tried to stem its flow.

"Soon after I arrived I searched for you, but you were nowhere to be found. I... I..." Should I tell her who I had found instead and what she had said? I was about to, remembering that we were confidantes, but then I stopped myself – what could I say? That I stumbled in upon your mother; that she is not only ill, she is a ruined thing; that I touched her hand, and when I did, it was as if I were a part of her? It would sound like nonsense. It *was* nonsense, my mind clearly overwrought due to recent events.

"I am so glad you are safe," I said, hugging her again.

How she humoured me that day, rushing to tell me all that had happened since our last meeting, and all that was planned for us during this one. Much of her chatter centred around James, as I knew it would, although she had only managed to rendezvous with him on one occasion since our visit to the tearoom, when she had been able to give her carriage driver, who doubled as her chaperone, the slip.

"He has become my shadow," she said, wrinkling her nose as she referred to the latter. "He believes himself to be so clever, but guess what?"

"What?" I loved how enthusiastic she was.

"I am wilier! I managed to lose him in the crowds and that is when I met with James."

It was such a daring thing to do, so... improper. My face must have betrayed my thoughts for she laughed uproariously.

"Oh Rosamund," she declared. "Dear, innocent Rosamund. A woman must take the reins of her life as if it is a tune; she must conduct it."

"Even though society demands something different?"

"It is *men* who say otherwise, but not all; not James; he is enlightened, a radical. That is how he describes himself. I want to be radical too."

Whereas all *I* wanted was to be normal.

"Constance, I worry for you. Your father…"

"Worrywart! You are not to, especially about him."

Her smile became coquettish as she sprung to her feet, a movement that caused her to stagger slightly.

"Constance," I enquired, "are you quite well?"

"I…I'm quite well, thank you," she replied, brushing yet another of my concerns aside. "I am going to call for the maid, she can help you to dress. Now listen here, be as quick as you can, for we have another exciting day ahead."

"Have we?" I asked, excitement beginning to grow in me too, outweighing everything else I was feeling. "What are we to do?"

"Take in more of London life, of course," she answered, heading for the door. "Oh, and pay a visit to a certain tea-room."

As her laughter again filled the air, I tried to smile also.

* * *

We had endless funds at our disposal, or at least according to Constance we did. She insisted that my father had sanctioned such extravagant spending – the commissioning of yet more dresses, more gloves, more hats. As for

Constance's father, she had declared him 'the richest man in the world', something I could not help but wonder at. Indeed, if my strange visions had any accuracy, the house in which they lived had not originally belonged to him but to her mother, therefore wasn't it *Helena's* riches that Constance alluded to? But now Helena was a prisoner at the townhouse, a very sick one. Just what was her illness exactly? Did Arthur have independent funds?

How could I begin to ask my friend these kinds of questions? Even to hint at them would surely dent her happiness in some way; it would steal the shine from her. What a thing to be responsible for! *Enjoy the day, Rosamund, stop thinking!*

I strove to do just that. With the carriage driver – a burly man in a long coat and a tall hat – keeping a respectable distance, we joined others in parading the busy thoroughfare, Regent Street being the name of it, and it was apparently the very hub of fashion. This was not difficult to believe as it was filled from end to end with gentlemen and ladies' outfitters, but in amongst them were also jewellery shops and perfumers, as well as one or two bakeries selling a range of delicious cakes and biscuits that you could take home with you in fancy boxes, each of them adorned with a festive ribbon. It had been a bright morning but during the afternoon the light was quick to fade. No matter in a city such as this; gas lamps came on swiftly, joined by the yellow glow of electrical light from a few of the more luxurious shops and hotels. It was breathtaking, all quite breathtaking. I felt giddy with delight.

The roads were crammed with black carriages such as the one the Lawton family owned and on the streets people jostled past, their faces red with cold and excitement. Soon it would be Christmas. An event I was not much given to, for why would I be? It was barely acknowledged at Mears House, Father sometimes being at home for the occasion, but in more recent years, not. Even should he be home, there would be little time spent with me – joyful time that is, rather than time spent interrogating. I shook my head at such a thought. Had there ever been such a thing as joyful time between us? Not that I could recall. And so Christmas Day had always been just like any other – one on which I passed the time reading or drawing, paying no heed to it. But here – in London – the atmosphere fizzed with anticipation.

Having walked the length of Regent Street, we came to a large open thoroughfare named Piccadilly Circus, escaping the crowds momentarily by taking a quiet, mainly residential, side road, before turning left and arriving at a garden square. There, another vision stopped me in my tracks.

"It is a tree," I breathed.

"Correct," Constance replied. "A Christmas tree."

A thing of splendour, it stood as tall as any of London's townhouses and was festooned with ribbons – red and green and gold in colour.

A Christmas tree – I repeated the words to myself. I had never seen such a thing, only having read of its history in one of the broadsheets that Father occasionally brought home, which included a description of the tree that Prince Albert had installed at Windsor Castle; and yet here one stood, before my eyes, even more magical than electrical light.

I could not say a word. I could barely breathe. But I could listen, and so I did, to the sweet voices of a huddled group who stood at the foot of the tree with pamphlets in their hands, from which they sang – "carols", Constance informed me, as I had not heard them before either, their voices swooping from note to note.

"What is this place?" I asked at last.

"This is Berkeley Square," she answered, "one of London's finest. And see over there, the fountain, how pretty it is?"

It was indeed, with its sparkling beads of water, but I could not bear to avert my gaze for too long from the tree. "May we go a little closer?"

"Of course!" she replied, taking my arm and practically pulling me along.

We stood close to the singers, who by now had begun another carol, one that referenced a 'good king' with an unusual name, Wenceslas, perhaps? I could almost reach out and touch the tree, we were so close, but I was a little afraid that if I did it might ruin the magic; might make it disappear. *What do you see?* Such wonders! Such magic! How could I have not known that this existed?

There and then I decided: I never wanted to return to Mears House, ever, despite Josie being there.

"We must go for tea soon," Constance said, giving me a moment to contemplate the prospect of detaching myself from such a marvellous sight.

"Yes, yes, of course," I returned, doing my utmost to commit every detail to memory lest the worst happened and I should never see its like again.

"Before that, though, I…I'll get us some roasted chestnuts."

Her voice sounded slightly odd, a little slurred as Father's was sometimes slurred, so I turned my head slightly to look at her. "Roasted chestnuts?"

She looked perfectly fine, if anything she was more beautiful than ever.

"There is a seller, just over there," she said, "by the fountain. I shall buy us some. You really must try them; it is quite the thing to do at this time of year. Although not too many, I cannot have you spoiling your appetite for later. Stay here, won't you?"

"Yes, yes, of course I will."

Left to my own devices, time seemed to stand still as I gazed about me, listened, and breathed in the smells that wafted on the air – smells quite unknown to me – the roasted chestnuts perhaps, earthy and pungent. When someone began tugging at my sleeve, I was surprised. Who would do such a thing? I looked down, it was Harry, I was sure of it – an urchin boy with a beautiful face and worldly eyes.

"Harry?" I said, to which he nodded. "Oh my," I exclaimed. "It is you!" I had wondered if I should see him again but had doubted it, London being such a huge place. "How are you? Are you well?"

When he declined to answer, I nodded towards the tree. "Is it not wonderful? I can barely believe my eyes. Living in London you must have seen a Christmas tree before, but this is my first time. I know, it is hard to believe, but I assure you, it is so. I just… It truly is wonderful. Harry, Harry, talk to me, why will you not speak?"

Still he refused. He simply continued to stare at me, but his face was beginning to change; it was becoming more shadowed. What with? Concern? He let go of my coat and pointed at my purse instead. I was confused at first and then I remembered, my necklace was in there, but how could he know?

Now, not just pointing, he began to jab at my purse, the action becoming decidedly more frenzied. A little afraid, I tried to seek Constance in the distance. There she was, by the fountain as she had said, in a queue for the roasted chestnuts. It looked as if she would be some time yet. What did this boy want – to steal the necklace from me? I had read of pickpockets, London was notorious for them. Was he one? Was such beauty, such innocence, deceiving?

"You cannot have it, Harry," I said sternly. "It is my necklace."

He shook his head. Wildly, he shook his head.

In the background the carol singers had started yet another song, one more sombre than the last: *Silent night, Holy night*. My unease was growing. No one knew what was in my pocket. Not even my friend, not yet.

Constance had instructed me to stay on the spot, but I began to back away from Harry. He followed me, matching me step for step, his eyes round, pleading almost. I picked up pace, determined to escape him, my hand covering my purse protectively. I could not lose the necklace; I had so little of my mother's, which made it all the more precious. I turned from Harry, hoping yet again to sight Constance, but failing miserably. Where was she? Where was I? I could not see the outline of the square anymore; all I could see were people, so many of them and more than before; far more. I was certain of it.

And some are just shadows.

The more I stared, the more I realised how true that statement was. And yet we had been lucky with the weather, it was a clear night with no mist to obscure the wonders we had seen. The people milled to and fro, the shadows too, but not all of them. Some had come to a standstill, were turning their heads towards me, their eyes widening with something akin to recognition. Why that should be so, I did not know. They were all strangers to me, every last one of them. One broke away from a group that were standing together, a man, his age quite indeterminable, but if I were to guess, I should say around thirty or so. He was a grizzled man with a long beard, his hat at an angle as if someone had accidently knocked it; his clothes not the clothes of a gentleman. Although his outline was hazy, his eyes were not; they reminded me of someone else's eyes – someone much closer to home; Father's! I did not know the word back then to describe the look in them, but I know it well enough now – malevolence – that was what they contained.

Like Harry, he did not need to open his mouth to speak. *Who are you? What are you?* Vividly, such words imprinted themselves on my mind.

Helena Lawton had asked the same thing. *I am normal*, I wanted again to say it, to scream it. *And you are not. You are far from normal.*

Harry had resumed tugging at my sleeve.

Although I could barely tear my gaze from this man advancing towards me, I felt I must. What Harry had to say was important.

He started jabbing at my purse again. Without questioning further, I reached in to retrieve the necklace – a talisman, a barrier – an heirloom.

Protection.

That was the message Harry wanted to impart – a timely reminder.

The man was now almost upon me. Although a

shadow, he was darker than nightfall; darker than any of the corridors in Mears House.

I held up the necklace and thrust it out before me, as if a shield, but it was all too much.

I began to sway on my feet.

Had it worked, had it stopped him?

That was all I could think as my body crumpled to the ground.

Chapter Eleven

"BUT, Father, I do not think she is well enough."

"She has to be, everything is set for tonight."

"She cannot be moved. Not yet."

"It has all been so carefully planned."

"What has?"

"She is to be presented."

"Presented where? Father, what is it you are trying to say?"

There was a silence and I found myself relishing it, drifting backwards, seeking solace somewhere deep in the back of my mind. It did not last long, however. The man was speaking again, not the female, and his voice was troubled.

"If… if she is not to be presented… when so much effort… It would be a disaster. There may be repercussions."

"Is it something I can help you with, Father?"

I wanted to shake my head at this, to shout *No!* Although why I wanted to do so quite so passionately, I could not fathom. Moreover, it would have been impossible. My head felt rigid, as though it were caught in a vice, and my mouth was woolly.

"You… You are not the same as Rosamund, Constance."

So it was Constance that was talking, although her

voice sounded different, having a distant quality, as if she was at one end of a tunnel and I at the other. The man she was conversing with was Arthur.

"We are not so different," she contradicted.

"Do you have any idea why she fainted?"

"None at all. I was queuing to buy some roasted chestnuts, I heard a commotion, looked over my shoulder and she was on the ground. Although… there was something… For a moment I thought I saw…"

When she faltered, Arthur prompted. "You were saying?"

"Oh nothing, nothing. A ruffian, I thought I saw a ruffian close to her, but in the blink of an eye he was gone. Perhaps I imagined it."

"London is full of ruffians."

"It is, Father, it can be. Do you think we should ask the doctor to visit? Her skin seems to be even more devoid of colour."

"We have everything she needs here. She will recover soon, but sadly not soon enough. Damn this accident! Why did you not keep a closer watch?"

"Father," Constance's voice held such indignation. "I was steps away!"

"But how can someone just faint?"

"It was cold, there were lots of people. All this is new to her – the city, the crowds, the sheer noise and excitement. Clearly she was overcome. I could not have foreseen it and I don't suppose she could have either. Father, wait! I think she may be stirring."

There was indeed the sound of someone moaning – was it me? Again, I seemed so detached from the situation – a spectator rather than a part of it.

Someone was by my side. They had taken my hand and proceeded to stroke it. The touch was light, reassuring. It must be Constance; his touch – Arthur's – would not engender such feelings, not after what his wife had said.

Mad… worse, evil.

Arthur, Father too, that man in the crowds… The latter in particular I could not bring myself to think of, not just now, I was not strong enough. I felt weak, longing for another touch, that of Josie's hand, or that of the mother I had never known. The necklace, where was my necklace…

Constance was speaking again.

"Should her father be here to see to her?"

"I have told you, he is otherwise engaged."

"He is drunk, you mean."

She was so bold! Evidently, her father thought so too.

"You are a fine one to talk regarding vices," he growled.

"Me?" The innocence in her voice was far from convincing. "What tales has the driver been telling you now?"

"You think you are so clever."

"If I am, I take after you, surely?"

"Constance—"

"You are afraid of him, aren't you?"

Afraid of whom? Were they still talking about my father?

"I am curious. What hold does Mr Howard have over you?"

"You ask too many questions."

"Like Mother? What a relief it must be for you then, that now she asks for one thing and one thing only."

"CONSTANCE!"

Arthur's raised voice startled me, almost bringing me fully back to consciousness, but before it did, I found myself slipping again. Even so, part of me silently pleaded with Constance: *do not goad him. Please, do not.*

Constance was her father's girl, she had told me herself on several occasions; she could wrap him around her little finger. But did she know him; truly know him, the way that her mother knew him? Did she realise what he was capable of – destruction in other words, of the human spirit. And was my father capable of that too? *My* spirit?

To my surprise, I sensed no cowering from Constance at Arthur's roar, rather she laughed, that lovely tinkling sound. If she *was* afraid of her father, she did not allow it to show and my heart swelled with love for her because of it. How brave she was, how plucky – everything I aspired to be. This was a woman who would change the world in a trice if she could; who would break free of all convention; who would bend the rules without hesitation to suit her own wishes.

But then a niggling remembrance – what did Arthur mean when Constance accused Father of being a drunk? He had said 'You are a fine one to talk regarding vices.' I remembered her staggering briefly, the morning she had come to fetch me for our outing, and then when we were out… *Dig deep, Rosamund, try and remember more…* In the queue for the roasted chestnuts, she had taken something from her purse, something secreted as my necklace had been secreted – a bottle it looked like – and, unscrewing the top, had popped a few drops of something onto her tongue. Although captivated by the Christmas tree I had wondered at it – was it a tincture of some sort, to treat the onset of a cold perhaps? Although she had not been snuffling or blowing her nose beforehand. Readily, I had dismissed it. It would not be anything harmful, not if she was taking it in public; she would not be so brazen.

But this was the thing with Constance – she believed she could do anything without consequence, not just bend the rules but live beyond them too.

"Father," she had long since stopped stroking my hand and I think had risen to meet her father eye to eye. "*I* want to be the one to be presented."

"I have told you, Constance, no."

"You have said that she is different, implying that I am not. Father, I *am* different. I want to be a part of what you are a part of." When still he made no reply, she continued. "I am not like Mother; I am not weak. And... and... I'm not afraid. Father, please, just listen to me. I think I know what you mean when you say that she is different. She has told me, you see, what she saw when she first came here; a woman at the window waving at her. A woman that does not *live* here."

What was it Constance was trying to say? The woman I had seen; who could she be if she did not live at the Lawton townhouse? A visitor, perhaps?

"Constance, the work the society carries out is highly valuable. We are at the very start of it; we are pioneers. If we do it correctly, our names will live on in history. But... there are dangers involved. Real dangers. I do not want you exposed to them."

But it was acceptable to expose *me*? My father had readily sanctioned that?

Again, I moaned, but this time no one came to my aid.

"Father, sometimes I can see too. I glimpse something, just like I have told you, you know, such as the ruffian, and then the next minute it is gone. The things I see are just... I don't know how to describe them. Shadows, I suppose.

Lately, it has been happening more and more."

Shadows?

"This is because of that substance you insist on taking," Arthur replied; "that your mother crams down her throat too."

What substance?

"I am curious, that is all, merely curious. Father, I *am* like you. I need to know everything there is to know in this world and if there is a world beyond, then why not learn about that one also? Present me tonight. Let me help in Rosamund's stead."

I could still sense his hesitance and prayed for him to refuse his daughter's request, I wanted neither of us exposed to whatever work it was they were involved with. She might not be afraid, but I certainly was.

Her final words, however, wore him down.

"You have admitted yourself that after all the trouble that has been gone to, if no one is presented, there may be repercussions. I rather think Mr Howard will ensure that is so. Surely then, it would be better to take a chance on me than to risk that?"

Oh Constance!

In that moment, my heart broke for her.

Chapter Twelve

I do not know how long I lay in that bed, whether it was for hours or days, but my mind refused to clear. Liquid that was both sweet and spicy had been delivered to my lips on several occasions. I had tried to fight it off, but to no avail. The hands that administered it – wizened hands – were stronger.

What medicine was this? Where was Constance? Crucially, what had happened to my necklace? Had she retrieved it when I had fallen? Was it once more safely ensconced somewhere, waiting to be found yet again?

And who was it that kept creeping into my room at night? For that was what they were doing – creeping, furtive in their actions, to stand over me. Was it Father? If so, he did not touch me; he came nowhere near. Only the person administering the medicine came close to me – was that Nell, the person who tended to Helena also?

Shadows – they also came creeping in. I would refuse to look at them, but they would find their way into my dreams regardless.

How that man troubled me, the one I had seen in Berkeley Square who had noticed me staring; whose eyes had grown wider, looking somehow lascivious. But he was not present in my dreams, nor were any of the other shadows I had seen whilst on the streets of London. They were, however, just as mysterious. They seemed to writhe in front of me, some of them reaching out as if they were begging for help, but others… Those others wanted no such thing. I have often mentioned that I could be beset by nightmares, but it was never more so than when I was at the townhouse. They were relentless, the medicine I was taking perhaps responsible for plunging me back down into subterranean depths again and again. But then I heard screaming and that pulled me upwards, all the way upwards.

There was such horror in it, such disbelief. *What have you done? You monster!*

Was that Constance shouting? No, the voice was different, yet I still recognised it.

"Be quiet, woman! I have told you, shut your mouth!"

Harsh words, but she obviously refused to obey.

"I knew that you would not stop at me; that you would destroy her too. For God's sake, when is enough enough?"

"It is my work!"

"It is your greed!"

"I am warning you—"

"You had plenty. You took it all from me, but no more, do you hear? No more! I will be subdued no longer. Your soul is damned. You have played with fire and it has burnt you." There was a sudden keening and that too was familiar to me. "My poor Constance! Oh, my darling girl! What have you done, Arthur? What have you done?"

Before Arthur could answer, there was a further shriek. "What is he doing here? No! No! I do not want him here! Get him out of my house, for he has darkened it further. He has led you as once you led me – all the way into Hell. You are weak, Arthur, you are so damned weak. Mark my words; the devil will destroy you just as you have destroyed your own family. What you toy with you do not understand, for that is what you do; you *toy* with it, thinking you know so much when you do not. It is referred to as the unknown for a good reason; we are not *meant* to know! At first, so much is promised, but never is it delivered. Evil is able to bide its time; it is a patient thing, but at the moment it chooses, it will pounce; it will destroy you and I shall be glad of it. You deserve an eternity of suffering for what you have done."

Where was all this commotion coming from? In my bedroom or just outside it?

I will be subdued no longer.

Constance's mother – for that was whom this voice belonged to – was clearly no longer that pitiful thing lying in bed, begging a complete stranger for yet more medication. She was on her feet, and she was screaming, yelling and demanding. For her to do that, something catastrophic must have occurred.

I had to emulate her, force myself from the stupor I was in; no longer exist amongst the shadows, but return to the living, who were just as frightening.

"Constance," I was shocked at how weak I sounded. "Constance, are you there?" How I hoped she was; how I prayed. Having managed to sit upright, I swung my legs over the side of the bed. I pushed them further, unsure whether I could support my own weight. With my feet on the rug, I staggered forwards, my actions reminding me of something I had seen as a child in one of the fields close to Mears House – a foal, just born, rising to its feet, minutes old; legs splaying outwards, threatening to buckle, and trembling, but how determined that foal had been, gradually gaining momentum. I was just as determined. If anything had happened to Constance; if she was in danger... *Constance is lost.* What did that mean? What could it possibly mean?

"Control your wife."

This was Father's voice and immediately Arthur responded.

"Go back to bed, Helena! Do not lecture on what you know nothing about."

The closer I drew to the source of their voices, the more I realised how tense the atmosphere was; as taut as copper wiring. They were not on the landing but in a room just opposite, and that door was open. Was it another bedroom? I was not sure, but I crept through the dimness, towards candlelight that flickered.

Three figures were in the room. As expected it was a bedroom but not Constance's, or Helena's; theirs' were on the third floor. A guest bedroom perhaps, Father's even? Continuing to peer through the door opening, I could see Arthur and Helena facing each other, both shaking but with very different emotions – Helena with anger, Arthur with a combination of that and fear. And there was Father, standing there, glaring at them.

"What happened—"

"What happened was an accident," Arthur was emphatic. "Do you think I would have hurt her, deliberately hurt her? She was my daughter!"

Was?

"You are a monster," Helena repeated, her voice giving way to sobs. "Oh, dear God, what is to become of us now?" Quickly she gathered herself. "You *are* a monster, Arthur, but one driven purely by greed. He, however..."

She jabbed a finger at my father, "is driven entirely by something else. Insanity."

To my increasing horror, Helena ran forward and threw herself at my father, her hands held before her, seemingly ready to claw him to pieces.

"Helena!" Arthur was screaming, but once more she refused to obey him. Constance had said she was not like her mother, but it seemed her mother was not as feeble as she had believed. This woman was attacking my father. My heart raced as I witnessed it; the blood rushing through my veins. Arthur had lunged forwards too but was seemingly finding it difficult to grab hold of his wife as her hands were flailing wildly.

"Helena, you must stop!" he continued. Besides desperation, there was worry in his voice; genuine worry, I was sure of it. But still she screamed as she scratched at my father who had to raise his hands to shield his face.

But then the scene changed abruptly. Father reached out and there was a snap, as loud as I imagined a gunshot to be. There followed a brief silence then a thud.

Helena Lawton's body hit the ground, jerking like one of the creatures from my nightmares before becoming still, her head lying at an unnatural angle.

Hurriedly, I stepped back not wanting to bear witness to any more heinous acts, but then sensed movement at my side. Was it Nell, the butler or another servant, come to see what all the drama was about? I felt angry. What had taken them so long? If only they had come sooner. They may have been able to save her!

It was not them. It was Constance. Her beautiful raven hair was no longer smooth and shiny, secured neatly with ribbons, but ragged around her head, as if she had been pulling at it in a frenzied manner, trying to tear it from her scalp. Her mouth was wide open and her eyes... Was it blood surrounding them, as if she had been trying to tear them out too? It was a terrible sight, yet strangely I was relieved to see her.

"Constance!" I said, reaching for her; trying to pull her close, to comfort her. Had she seen what I had – her mother murdered, by none other than my father?

All I grasped was thin air as Constance faded clean away.

My subsequent screams rivalled any that Helena had been capable of.

* * *

"She is coming round; she is awake."

Were the voices referring to me? Had I fainted again? That smell that assaulted me – sweet but sickly, the oddest perfume – what was it?

I opened my eyes but there was only darkness. If my head had hurt before, it hurt even more so now. What had happened to cause this? For a moment all was blank.

And then a light flickered, one candle followed by several others. I counted them as they were lit, including the one in front of me; there were thirteen in total.

I was in a room, and I was far from alone – there were men, so many of them. I continued counting, perhaps desperate to keep my mind occupied and try to make sense of what was happening; twelve men, plus me – thirteen again.

We were sitting around a table and I was upright, not

by my own efforts; I was restrained it seemed by leather cuffs.

"All is well," one of the men assured me. "We mean you no harm."

"That is right," another man said, again a stranger, "we only seek your help."

"Rosamund, listen to my colleagues. And cooperate."

My head swung towards the man who had last spoken. It was Father, and beside him was Arthur, who was sitting with his head bent and his hands clasped together.

Quickly, I tried to calculate where I was – as far as I could tell it was a wood panelled room with some artwork on the walls. There was also a sideboard and a rather ostentatious mantelpiece, two candelabras set at each end. A drawing room then, but at the townhouse or another address? "Where am I?" I was forced to ask.

"At a private residence," another stranger answered.

"The Lawton house?"

"Not there," the same man replied. "Please relax, we will explain what we can."

I baulked at that. "What you can? What can you *not* explain?"

The man who was doing the majority of talking glanced at my father, there was an irritation in him, but it was mild compared to that which emanated from Father.

"Rosamund," he hissed. "Quieten down."

"Another like Constance," someone else said, I did not catch who.

"Wilful," another agreed.

"More Laudanum perhaps?"

Laudanum? What was that?

"No." It was a young man with fair hair speaking this

time; someone vaguely familiar. "Drugs should not be permitted. They…" briefly he faltered, "…skew the results. If we influence the subject with laudanum, then how can we expect our society to be taken seriously?"

A general murmur ensued, filled with the comments of those who agreed and disagreed. 'Drugs are useful; they open the doors of the mind. It has been demonstrated' and 'yes, we must strive for accreditation not against it.'

"Please, gentlemen," the young man seemed to have grown bolder, "no laudanum and no…" here he took a deep breath, "other devices either." Before Father could respond, the young man's eyes were back on me. There was a gentleness to him that was missing in every one of the others, and, dare I even think it – as he himself clearly contributed to the terrible circumstances in which I found myself – a kindness? He attempted a smile. "If Rosamund's ability is genuine, as Mr Howard insists that it is, then surely there is no need."

"It *is* genuine," Father hissed again, and I found myself thankful that he was not standing close to this young man with a poker in his hand, for unlike me he would use it. My head reeling, my senses on fire, I begged for yet more information.

"Who are you? What do you want with me? What is this ability to which you refer? I do no understand. I do not!"

Another man spoke, one that was sitting directly opposite me at the round table, the wavering candlelight first revealing his face then concealing it by turn.

"We are the founder members of the *Society of the Rose Cross*, a magical organisation devoted to the study and practice of the occult, metaphysics and paranormal activity.

We draw upon many influences not least Kabbalah, Astrology, Tarot, Geomancy and Alchemy. Sitting amongst us today, you will find doctors, gentlemen and scholars. There is great interest amongst our peers in the spiritual world, but sadly, many treat it without the deference it deserves. Séances, table tipping and mediumship are all considered parlour games. In contrast, our society treats the subject with the utmost respect. We seek to learn from it, and in learning, evolve. Making contact with the spiritual world is an area we focus on. Our aim is to *prove* its existence, something we believe you may be able to help us with."

"Me?" I gasped, trying to make sense of all this man was saying. Some of the words he had used – Geomancy, Alchemy, and Tarot – he may as well have been speaking in a foreign tongue. "How could I possibly help you to prove that?"

"Because you can see."

Again I baulked, struggling against my restraints.

What do you see?

All the times my father had said that to me during my lifetime; it went back years, to when I was but a small child. Running; I was always running away from him, always trying to escape. How I wanted to escape now; to flee from this room and its strange occupants. But I could not. All that it was in my power to do was answer the man as I have always answered Father. "All I see is what you can see too."

My father jumped to his feet, a sudden action accompanied by the banging of his fist on the table, making me flinch and several others around him, I noticed.

"You *can* see, Rosamund! Your ability is genuine, the

pictures, all those pictures…" He looked at the men instead of me. "You are right, laudanum can dull the senses, rather than enliven them, I accept that, but this other drug, this new drug, it is different; it prevents lying; the doctors amongst you can pay testament to that. And this child, oh how she will lie. She is adept at it; she is cunning; she will deny all that she is capable of, time and time again. Her mother was the same. If only I had had the drug then…" Anguish caused him to clench his fists. "I urge you all to agree that we use it on Rosamund, here, tonight, in this room. Laudanum has not yielded the results I wanted. It will be easy enough to send someone in a carriage to fetch it. Gentlemen, please, are you not tired of waiting? I know that I am."

The man who had introduced the society to me stood too. "We will do no such thing! Stephen is right, if it is found that drugs have been used in our research, it will devalue everything we do. It will tarnish our reputation, perhaps irrevocably. Now sit, William, and allow me to continue." When Father refused to do so, the man's glare tightened. "You will sit, or you will take your leave."

"If I do, that will break the chain," Father retorted.

"So be it."

There followed several moments of harsh silence with Father still standing and the man continuing to glare at him. I wanted Father to carry on with his rebellion; to break the chain, whatever the chain was, then perhaps I could go free too, but gradually he succumbed, lowering himself into the chair beside Arthur.

Satisfied, the man also sat before addressing me once more. "My name is Andrew Griffin; Arthur Lawton you have previously met and of course, there is your father.

Allow me to introduce the other members of the society to you; there is David Woodbridge, Sir Samuel McPherson, Alan Mathers, Stephen Davis…" On and on the list went, all the way up to twelve.

"And you, Rosamund Howard, are our thirteenth guest; our most esteemed guest, a guest who has the power of sight, and who I am hoping will enable us to see too."

Violently I shook my head. "Please. I only wish to go home." To Mears House; to Josie – to run into her arms; to take refuge in the attic; to hold my mother's picture against my breast; to imagine her arms around me too. I was the same as her apparently; did that mean Father thought she could see also?

Perhaps he is right, Rosamund; after all, you have seen Constance, Harry, the man on the street, all those shadows…

No! Imagination! It was pure imagination, or fever!

I had seen other things I had never expected to see either; electrical light; the Christmas tree, bedecked in ribbons; the rosy-cheeked glow of women in long flowing skirts and tall handsome men in suits and top hats – glorious sights, sights to warm the heart, not frighten it or leave it stone cold.

"Rosamund," Andrew Griffin's voice interrupted such thoughts. "We would like you to demonstrate, that is all."

"You are forcing me to demonstrate. You have trussed me up!"

"For your own safety." He turned to his colleagues. "Gentlemen, I believe it may be easier to see in the darkness. Please, one by one, blow out your candles, following my lead. We will go in a clockwise motion."

What was this? I was to be plunged into darkness?

"Let me go!" I shouted. "I cannot see anything. I will

not!"

"What do you see, Rosamund?" Griffin uttered despite my protests, the light from his candle dying.

"What do you see, Rosamund?" the man next to him, David Woodbridge, said in turn, before snuffing his candle out too.

"What do you see, Rosamund?" This was McPherson; then it was Mathers; then Davis… the room growing darker and darker, becoming filled with shadows.

"I see nothing!" The shadows were merely that, although… distorted by what remained of the candlelight, they were beginning to loom… to take shape.

"What do you see, Rosamund?"

"Nothing! Nothing!"

"What do you see, Rosamund?"

Soon it would be Father's turn to ask it.

"What do you see, Rosamund?"

The pictures, all those pictures…

What had Father meant by that?

"What do you see, Rosamund?"

There was yet more darkness, yet more shadows. As on the streets of London, the room was crammed with them. I shut my eyes but I knew it to be in vain; as in the bedroom at the townhouse, such shadows could permeate everything.

"What do you see, Rosamund?"

Harry – I would like to see Harry; such a beautiful face he had, and those eyes of his that looked like they had lived a thousand years – or been dead a thousand years? Again, I shook my head at where that thought had led me. *No! No! No!*

"What do you see, Rosamund?" That was my father's

voice, a growl in it.

"Stop it! All of you stop it!"

A voice beside my own began to speak, concern in it; the voice of the young man, Davis? If so, he was easily overruled.

The girl at the window, waving to me; who was she? I had not seen her within the townhouse, and why would she be waving, trying to gain my attention?

The twelfth man to ask me the same question would be Arthur.

Oh, Constance. I saw you. I saw you and yet you were dead…

That firm realisation caused my heart to plummet and my mouth to gape open. But they were not *my* screams that filled the air. Not this time.

They belonged to Arthur.

Chapter Thirteen

"MY daughter, my darling daughter, my wife... What have I done? What have *we* done? Their blood is on my hands. Look! Look at them! Can you see? They are dripping with blood!"

"Light the candles, all of you," someone commanded. "Quickly, light them."

"Arthur! Arthur! What are you doing, man? Calm down!"

"Light the candles, damn it!"

As the commotion continued, I struggled against my cuffs, determined to undo them; to escape, but to no avail. I was held fast, stuck in the midst of pandemonium.

There was light now, the men obeying the command of Griffin, and the shadows receded as those who were really present in the room came into full view.

Arthur Lawton had gone mad. That is what it appeared. He was on his feet and his hands were in front of him, his eyes bulging with horror and his mouth wide open as he continued to scream; to insist there was blood on them.

"Oh dear Lord, we killed them, didn't we, William? You and I."

Men were rushing towards him but he appeared to have a strength that was inhuman, throwing them from him as though they were rag dolls.

"Arthur!" I was unable to identify who it was beseeching him again. "You need to remain calm!"

More men approached him, warily this time. I needed desperately to escape. I had seen no door ahead of me or to my side and concluding that it must be behind me, I began to push with my feet, making my chair scrape and bump in that direction.

Still Arthur was screaming. "Constance! We killed Constance!"

"Arthur, what happened was not our fault!" It was Griffin insisting this.

"She was an addict," insisted another. "You never divulged that. If we'd known… That is why it must be the correct decision to ban the use of substances with our subjects from hereonin, because contrary to what has been said, they do not dull a person, but they *do* open doorways, which at our stage of development is dangerous."

"What she saw…" Arthur's voice was as pitiable as his wife's had once been.

"Was hallucination," Griffin rushed to answer. "It had to be."

"She gouged at her eyes! To do that, to go to that length—"

"IT WAS MERE HALLUCINATION!" continued Griffin. "We have discussed this!"

Arthur's whimpers matched mine. "What if you are mistaken? My wife said I was evil, that I was damned. Perhaps I am: because of her, because of Constance—"

"Pull yourself together, man!" I recognised that growl as I continued to edge myself backwards. "Listen to Griffin! What happened to Constance was an accident. You should never have brought her here in the first place; I was astonished when you did – someone that did not have the sight; who merely fancied she did. What were you thinking, man? How could you be so easily duped, and by a chit of a girl too?"

"Constance is dead!" Arthur wailed.

"Yes, she is, but what is now important is that our society cannot be held accountable for it."

"What? Is that *all* that is important to you; to all of you? You… You bastard!"

Arthur lunged at my father, who, as he had done with Helena, immediately held up his hands in order to hold his opponent at arm's length.

"You killed my wife," Arthur twisted his head towards the others, who had rushed to help but now stood aghast at what was being said. "This man killed my wife. It was in my house; *my* house damn it. With his bare hands, he grabbed her neck; he snapped it, just as if it were a twig. He murdered her in cold blood."

"William?" It was Griffin asking, while the others clustered wide-eyed around him. "What he is saying, what he is… *accusing* you of, is there any truth to it?"

Father kept his eyes on Arthur as he answered. "I rather fear this man is every bit as addled as his daughter."

Arthur renewed his attempts to attack my father. "YOU KILLED HER!"

"WHERE IS THE PROOF?" Father returned. "You are deluded, sir!"

"I am the proof," I said, but my voice was lost in what ensued next.

Father suddenly lost his restraining grip on Arthur, who, seizing his chance, enclosed Father's neck with his hands and began to squeeze, squeeze, squeeze. A part of me egged him on, wishing… hoping… A part of me I refused to indulge further. Whatever he had done, whatever ills he had committed, William Howard was still my father, and I should be lost without him. I would be an orphan.

A group of the other men also joined in the struggle, trying to release Arthur's grip. In their efforts they knocked over a candle, causing the cloth that had covered the table to burst into sudden flames.

"What the deuce…?" someone shouted. "We need water. Quick! Water!"

Smoke filled the air with alarming rapidity, finding its way into my lungs and causing me to cough, choke, and making my eyes stream. Even more panicked, I bucked, still intending to free myself of what bound me and, as I did, the chair tipped backwards. I crashed to the ground, once more hitting my head. Mercifully, I did not lose consciousness; I could not afford to, not if the room was burning.

"Someone help me. I beg you, let me go," I whimpered.

There were so many voices, but the loudest of all was Arthur's. He continued to yell, seemingly taking no note of the fact that the room was alight. "He killed my wife, in front of my very eyes. He is a murderer, a filthy murderer!"

"Arthur! Arthur! We must leave. We will deal with William later. Come, Arthur, please!"

I did not know who said this, but if they were leaving, surely they would not leave without me? I was not oblivious to the flames as Arthur appeared to be; I did not want to suffocate or be incinerated. I could not imagine a worse way to go.

"Help! Help!"

They *were* leaving! There were trampling all over me to

escape. Why? How could they do such a thing?

"Father! Arthur! Help!"

It was a hideous sound that next met my ears; a cry filled with unimaginable pain. I could barely bring myself to look but I must – I could not hide or remain ignorant – not anymore.

One of the men was on fire. He was beating at his torso with frenzied hands, doing his utmost to battle the ravages of such a fierce element. It was Arthur, I was sure of it. Another man tried to help him – the young man I think, Stephen Davis, although his fair hair looked blackened. He attempted to beat the flames back with his bare hands, but as Arthur went careering into the wall, Davis had to admit defeat, although I could sense his anguish in doing so; his sheer disbelief. He stood there, his hands if not burnt, at least badly scorched, and I cried out once again. "Help! Help!"

My voice had become a mere croak, dying in my throat as I would surely die in this room if no one came to my aid. I could feel the heat of the fire searing my face; it was creeping closer, just like the shadows would creep, but soon it would do so much more than that; it would charge towards me, unrestrained, unstoppable, the strongest element of all. Unable to move, I began to sob. Yet again, I was defenceless.

"Help! Help!" I called one last time before shutting my eyes and resigning myself to such a hideous fate.

"Be calm, I have you."

My eyes snapped open.

"What? Who is this?"

"It's Stephen. I have you, Rosamund; we will escape this."

"Where... where is Arthur...?"

There was a moment of silence but it spoke volumes.

"Arthur is lost," he said at last.

As the other members of his family had been lost – all of them gone.

"I have to turn you onto your side, to untie you, I mean."

"Yes. Yes." I replied. "Please hurry."

"I will. We shall get you out, I promise. I am sorry... I just... I am so sorry."

He worked as quickly as he could to release me, enabling one of my hands to become free, followed by the other. I attempted to climb to my feet but my legs would not comply. Stephen must have noticed my difficulty for he put his arms around me and lifted me as though I were a child instead of a girl of sixteen, and together we began to make our way to the door, with the flames not only behind us, but leaping higher and higher on either side. How soon before the entire house burned?

Just as we reached the door, a figure shot forward.

"Unhand her!"

"Father?" I managed.

"I said, let her go! She is my daughter!"

Although the man holding me protested, he set me down. Father, however, was in no mood for remonstration – not this time. With both hands he gave Stephen a great shove and the young man fell backwards, into the flames.

"FATHER, NO! WHAT ARE YOU DOING?"

In no mood for explaining either, he grabbed my hand, his touch so unlike Stephen's; there was no gentleness in it at all as he dragged me forwards. I did my utmost to stop him, the one hand I had free holding onto the doorframe;

digging my heels into the floor; but this time I *was* a child, and my strength was no match for his.

"We cannot leave Stephen in there," I shouted as he continued to drag me down the hallway and out of the house, where quite a crowd had gathered, huddled in clusters as if watching live theatre. "Father, we cannot, he will perish!"

Just as Arthur had perished, as Helena had said he would, in the flames of Hell.

"FATHER!"

In spite of my protestations, he merely increased the distance between us and the crowds. I recognised some of the men who had been in the room. They were coughing and spluttering, and some had also noticed us. They were pointing towards Father, and calling out to him, trying to catch his attention. He simply lowered his head and bustled us both along, into what quickly became a warren of streets.

At last I recognised where we were; the crescent with its graceful curve.

"Why are we here?" I asked, my bewilderment increasing at once again seeing the Lawton family home. When he refused to answer, I cried out, attracting the attention of a passerby. "We cannot go back inside there, Father, we cannot."

"Be quiet, Rosamund!"

"Then tell me why."

"There is something I need to retrieve, that is why. Damn them," he seethed as we continued towards the house, "with their rules and their regulations, their *rigidity*. It is I that holds the key to it all. It is me that has you. Enough questions! Gather your things, Rosamund, and quickly. I will see to it that a carriage is waiting for us when you come downstairs. I warn you, do not dally. We have to leave London and soon."

He rapped on the door and the butler appeared, a scowl on his face at the sight of us, his commitment to his profession perhaps forcing him to hold his tongue. As we entered the hallway, Father issued instructions for transport to be hailed. Whilst he did, I looked about me. What a grand hallway this was in Helena's family home, which had been given over to her husband; stolen from her through marriage. An evil man, but he had loved his daughter at least; Constance had been right about that, the loss of her sending him mad, quite mad. Would he burn forever? I wondered. Would all of us burn in the end?

In the hallway, the gaslight flickered just as the candles had done at that other townhouse, casting shadow upon shadow. As I began to walk towards the staircase; as I stared at their ill-defined forms; they slowly began to move.

Chapter Fourteen

I was awake as I continued to climb the staircase. I knew that. This at least was not a dream. Even so, it appeared that dreams and reality had merged to produce a new version of reality; as though the barriers that had previously divided the two had come tumbling down, allowing so many and so much through.

This house where until today had lived an esteemed London family, was not empty; far from it, it was *full* of people: the fair-haired girl who had waved at me when I first came here but one of them. Like the streets outside, it was teeming; some figures passing blithely by me, passing *through* me even; others stopping to stare at the girl amongst them; curious about her; stretching a hand towards her.

I did not shrink back as I had done in Berkeley Square, or scream or faint – I think my senses had grown numb after all I had experienced in recent days. It was as if I had become unable to react; as though I was now a shadow too. What had happened to Stephen when Father pushed him backwards? What if he had…? No, I must not think that. Better to remain numb.

I did not stop at the crest of the first flight of stairs; I continued on to the second floor and then the third – the floor where I knew Helena's bedroom to be; compelled to go there and not questioning that compulsion, not yet. It was already dark outside but the corridor was darker still with no living person, no Nell, scurrying along the landing. Why would she be? Who was there now here to tend to?

Reaching Helena's room, I pushed open the door and the smell that assaulted me was the same as ever, sweet but sickly. Rather than the darkness, I focused on one thing and one thing only – that smell – closing my eyes and breathing it in, despite how repellent it was. Was this the smell of laudanum, the drug the society had referred to? If so, Helena had been an addict, though perhaps not at first; perhaps initially she had had an illness for which it had proved useful – indeed she had hacked blood up right in front of me, so that could be true. But still she had become addicted to whatever had dulled the pain; dulled her mind – *or opened doors.* Constance had had the same smell about her sometimes. It was only now, standing there, that I fully realised it, remembering how she too had staggered on occasion; how sometimes her words had been a little slurred, or her eyes perhaps over bright. *Drugs open the doors of the mind.* Constance had mentioned that she thought she had seen a ruffian close to me when I had fainted. Was that proof that he was real, or that her drug use had done exactly that: opened her mind? That same drug – laudanum – had been administered to me as I lay in bed on the first floor – I was now certain of it – not as a means to ease my pain but as an attempt to make me more pliable. If so, it was not the only drug that could do that, Father had said there was another; one that was more effective; that prevented lying…

Is that why we had had to return here, so that Father

could retrieve it?

As I was about to turn and leave the room – coming here having confirmed my suspicions about the nature of laudanum at least – a movement caught my eye. The bed – previously empty, was empty no more! Although all was silent in the room, I could hear the rush of blood – my own – as it coursed through my veins. *No! No! I do not want this.* Helena Lawton was dead. She should remain that way.

I hurriedly made to leave the room.

Constance is lost. I am lost.

Those were the words Helena had used, and – as if she had indeed had the gift of prophecy – she had been correct. A woman full of fun and enthusiasm, who had given birth to another similar to her, but was then lost to the darkness that her husband had plunged her into. But if it were Helena on this bed, she had *become* the darkness.

That thought was reinforced by something more she had said – *the light hurts.*

How could something as wonderful as the light hurt?

I was about to run down to my room, throw my belongings into the suitcase and go and meet Father, but I suddenly could not bring myself to do it. Not until there *was* light. Not daylight, not electrical light, but the only light there was at my disposal – gaslight. Seized with the desire to illuminate this dark, dark house, I rushed to the table with the candle, beside which would be kept a box of matches and wax tapers. I grabbed them, dragging the match head along the striking surface and watched as it burst into flame. There was nothing threatening about it this time; instead it was something beautiful; something valiant – *the strongest element of all*, that is what I had thought just an hour or two earlier; to be used for good, *only* for good; in this case for the purpose of cleansing. I then lit the taper and, making my way to the centre of the room, inserted it through the hole in the bottom of the globe in the ceiling gaslight. Tilting the chain, there was a popping sound as the gas ignited.

Watching it, I heard a roar in my head; a desperate protest.

Immediately I turned back towards the bed. "The light will not hurt you. Not anymore. There is no need to be afraid."

I took the matches and tapers with me as I left the room. The figure in the bed had, miraculously, quietened at my words; had, I think, *listened*.

In the hallway, I lit yet more lamps before rushing back down the stairs to my room, aware that I had to act quickly; that Father was waiting. All the while I addressed the shadows.

"You must not be afraid. Please. You need the light. The light will help."

Who was I reassuring? I wondered. Them or simply myself? I had no time to contemplate; the words *felt* right, that was all that mattered. I had to get to my room… via the one in which Helena was felled.

That room needed the light most of all.

My breathing was a harsh sound in my ears as I moved towards it. What would I encounter in there? Not just shadows but something more substantial; perhaps Constance herself, just as I had seen her in the corridor – her eyes, oh her eyes! Or it might be Helena again, not in bed this time, but standing with her head lolling.

Hold fast. Do not allow your imagination to take over.

Because some of it *was* imagination, I was sure of it. *Maybe all of it?*

I shook my head. No. Not all. *Do what you came here to do and light the lamp.*

My hands shaking violently now, I moved to the exact spot where Father had slain Helena, and, as I did, a terrible coldness seized me; it was worse than any winter chill; akin to the cold I had felt in the woods of Mears House that day, when I had fallen and Josie had appeared to take care of me.

What Father and Arthur had done with the body I had no idea, or how long the interval had been between the time I had blacked out and when I had been taken to that room where the society had gathered. However long it was, it was time enough for them to remove it. But what had they done with Helena? Was she lying in a ditch somewhere? Or at the bottom of that great river that snaked its way through London – the Thames, no doubt the resting place of many a wronged soul?

I corrected myself; even if her body lay there, it did not imply her soul did.

Light the lamp, Rosamund.

I did, leaving it to blaze behind me as I left the scene of the murder and entered my own room, where I lit another, this time for more practical reasons, so that I could see to pack. As I did, as the shadows became less and less, I noticed something: something glittering.

It was my necklace! Lying there on the floor in front of me!

Squatting, I snatched it up – terrified it might disappear if I did not act with haste.

I was certain it had not lain there before. I would have

sworn to it. It was in so blatant, so obvious a position, that it would have been impossible to miss.

The sound of laughter caused me to gasp – *tinkling* laughter.

"Constance?" I whispered, my head whipping from left to right. "Was it you? Did you keep it safe for me?"

And return it from the dead, my necklace and my protection.

"Rosamund! Where are you? Hurry! Our coach is waiting."

On hearing Father rather than Constance, I straightened up and did as before; placed the necklace in my purse. One day, though – and I promised myself this – I would wear it for all to see – my mother's necklace, and her gift to me.

"Rosamund!"

"I am coming, Father."

Throwing whatever I could into my suitcase, I forced it shut and retraced my footsteps. At the top of the stairs I came to a halt, turning to look behind me.

I saw nothing but light.

"Be at peace, Helena," I whispered. "And, Constance, my dear friend, rest well."

* * *

There is not much that I remember about the carriage ride home. Father sat opposite me, his breathing heavy as he sipped, sipped, sipped from a flask – the smell not as pungent as laudanum perhaps, but it was as sickly, and to combat it, I did my utmost to breathe only shallowly. Clutched in his hands was a carpetbag, what it contained the reason we had gone back to the house to fetch, no doubt. I glanced at him only briefly, trying to come to terms with what I now knew him to be – a murderer. Not only was I at his mercy, I was his descendant. His blood was my blood. If there was darkness in him would it follow that darkness existed in me too?

As we continued to travel over rough roads for what would be hours and hours, I had to remind myself that I was also a part of Mother. And although I had no living memory of her, because of the necklace I felt her presence near and she was good – wholly good. There was so much good in this world… and so much bad. And perhaps, just perhaps, there was a world within us all.

The dawn was breaking as at last we entered the grounds of Mears House. Father was sleeping, albeit fitfully, his body twitching occasionally, causing him to groan.

As the house came into view, I could not resist leaning forward. There it stood, the house in which I had been raised; the mausoleum, with nothing festive to brighten it, not even at Christmas. Inside were Miss Tiggs and Josie. Would they be surprised at our return, or were they expecting us? I would soon find out.

The driver brought the carriage to a halt, another jolt that this time succeeded in awakening Father.

"What is it? Have we arrived? Are we here?"

Rather than answer, I opened the carriage door, the driver helping me to step down. As Father alighted he missed a step and the driver hastened to help him too. Rather than accept, Father brushed his hands away, determined to right himself by his own efforts. Throughout he kept a tight hold on the carpetbag. *What is it you have in there?* Again I could not help but wonder.

Whilst he paid the driver, I turned to the house and once more took it all in; how many windows it had; how many eyes. Above it were only clouds and sky, the early morning colours not glorious but leaden. There were no birds, I noticed. There very seldom were. But not everything stayed away, not by far.

As the driver departed, and Father began to approach the house, I knew I had gained some sort of reprieve. He would need to sleep properly, not the fitful kind you snatched whilst journeying, but deep sleep, the kind that rejuvenated you. Whatever he planned now, he would want to do it properly, not on the back of exhaustion.

As we entered, Miss Tiggs was in her usual position on the inside of the door, although there was no sign of Josie. I hurried towards the staircase and began to climb, making my way not to the attic, but to my room, there to dig the necklace from my purse and hug it to me as I lay on the bed and prayed for sleep to find me too.

For in the coming hours, I would need all the strength I possessed.

Chapter Fifteen

"ROSAMUND, darling."

Darling? Who was calling me that? I cannot recall any person having used that term of endearment towards me, perhaps not even Constance.

"That's it, easy now," the voice continued. "It's me, Josie."

Josie? Had she dispensed with 'miss' completely?

It had been during the morning that I had fallen asleep, and I was so tired that I had foregone the drawing of the curtains. In spite of that, no daylight pervaded, instead the room had about it a hazy quality.

As I sat up I rubbed at my eyes. After a moment, panic set in.

"Don't worry about your necklace," Josie said, the smile upon her face soft rather than dazzling. "It's quite safe."

"How did you know…?" I began, but my voice soon trailed off.

Josie was sitting close to me, still with her red hair captured beneath her cap, but for those rogue wisps that tended to frame her face – heart-shaped I noticed it was, although for some reason that fact had evaded me until now. She was still pale; still with those glassy green eyes – the shine far more natural than that which had been in Constance's eyes. It seemed to reflect a quality from deep within and I found myself envying it. She appeared just as she always had, but there was also something new and different about her; something I could not quite identify.

"The stones in your necklace," she said, "do you know what they are?"

I shook my head. I had been meaning to ask Constance but had now missed the opportunity.

"Tourmaline. And Harry was right when he said what he did; they'll protect you. They will lend courage when you need it most."

"Josie," this time I refused to allow my voice to fail me. "How could you possibly know about the stones?"

She laughed. "Perhaps there's more to me than meets the eye."

I pondered on this before continuing. "And how do you know about Harry?"

"Because we are connected, Rosamund. All of us. That's how."

Instead of pondering further, it struck me quite suddenly what was different about Josie. Not only was she employing terms of endearment, her entire demeanour had changed. Gone was the simple country girl who would spend her life curtseying to others; she now had, if anything, an air of superiority about her. I leant forward but did not dare to touch her, my suspicion preventing me from doing so. "Who are you?" I whispered, not just experiencing bewilderment but many other emotions besides.

A bang at the door followed by the turn of the handle, caused us both to stare at it, instead of at each other.

Beads of sweat broke out on my forehead. "Is that Father?"

"No," Josie replied, her gaze still on the door. "But it will be soon."

"Who is it, then?" I asked, puzzled.

She turned back to me, taking my hand in hers and gripping it tight. "What you did at the townhouse, it was the right thing to do. You knew that, in spite of what Mrs Lawton had said. No one had to tell you. You drew upon instinct."

Was she referring to the gas lamps and the urge that overcame me to light them? But once again, how could she know this? "Is this another dream?"

She inclined her head a little. "It is perhaps a half dream."

I could not help but become a little angry at the vagueness of her replies, and as I did, the rattling at the door increased.

Rather than be alarmed by it, she smiled again. "See the power you have, Rosamund; *natural* power. Use it wisely."

I could not continue to sit. I snatched my hand from hers, leapt to my feet and began to pace as Father would pace. When I abruptly realised my actions were his, I came to a halt and turned to her, tears beginning to fall. I lifted my hand to touch them and it came away wet. How could this be a dream when tears felt real enough?

"I am afraid," I admitted.

"And where do you go when you're afraid?"

"The attic."

"The attic is safe?"

"Yes, yes it is."

Josie stood too. "How do you know it's safe?"

"Because... because..."

"Instinct tells you so?"

"Yes." It was another admission. "Instinct tells me so."

She reached out and once more held my hand. Her touch was gentle, extraordinarily so; a touch that only she was capable of.

"Trust in your instinct. Always."

I hung my head and allowed more tears to come – a wave that threatened to become tidal. The rattling had ceased completely now; there was no more banging, only the sound of my sobbing. "Josie, Josie," I wailed, as her arms encircled me, "I am so frightened. I am. What is he going to do with me?"

"There, darling, there. Let the tears wash away your grief."

Grief? Yes, that was *exactly* the emotion that I was feeling. Grief at what I had lost, and what I had never had.

A ray of light pierced the gloom. As I stood there with Josie's arms around me, sobbing into her shoulder, it caused me to open my eyes; to marvel at how bright it was; how daring, to venture into a dream as bleak as this.

Still I cried, continuing to relish the comfort of close contact. I cried for me, and I cried for Constance, I cried for Helena too, who had been weak and pitiful, but who had rallied at the end in defence of her daughter, and been killed as a consequence.

By Father.

"Oh, Josie," I whimpered. Did I have the strength in me to face the man that had sired me? Should I simply run from this room, not to the attic, but towards the woods in an effort to escape? But there was something waiting in the woods, I had seen it. Something within the house also, rattling the door…

There was no further comfort to be had and so I pushed

Josie away.

"No. I cannot do this. Something is happening here that I do not understand. I just... I want to be normal. I do not want this... any of it. Do you hear?"

When Josie failed to reply, I turned from her and faced the wall; I brought my hands up to my head and tugged at my hair. This dream, this nightmare, it was not populated with twisted creatures and writhing limbs as it usually was; it was just Josie and I, and yet still it was terrifying. I opened my mouth to scream, and scream I did, albeit silently. It was a purge nonetheless – allowing what was in me; what had been contained for so long – at least a degree of freedom.

Spent, I turned back to face this shimmering creature.

"You are not real, are you?"

Again she inclined her head. "I *am* real. But there's only some who can see me."

"A ghost?" I whispered.

"If you want to call me that. If it helps you to understand."

"I understand nothing!"

Her smile grew wider. "You are such a plucky little thing," she declared.

Plucky?

"I am weak," I insisted.

"You are strong, and you are strong because you are beginning to see."

What do you see?

"Miss Tiggs..." I said at last.

"Miss Tiggs died two years ago."

What? "But she has been here forever. I... I have seen her, talked with her, in the kitchen; sometimes at the front door, when she was bidding us, or rather Father, farewell."

"Has your father acknowledged her lately?"

I thought about it and then shook my head. No, I believe he had not.

"She never liked you, did she?" Josie said.

"I never liked her!"

"I don't think anyone did much. She could be selfish."

Could? "But I have seen her!" I reiterated. "A few hours ago I saw her. And as little as a week or two ago, I was sitting in the kitchen conversing with her whilst I ate supper."

She was silent, forcing me to speak again. "I conversed with a ghost?"

Slowly, she nodded.

"Just as I am doing now?"

There was another nod, and so I had to face the truth of the matter.

"It is only Father and I in this house." How solemn my voice was when I spoke these words. "And there has been for a long time. The governess…"

"Your Father wouldn't – *couldn't* – pay the fees."

"He has other matters that require his finances, what little remains of them."

Josie was quiet, allowing me to come to terms with it all.

It was just he and I in this big old crumbling house, set deep within the Sussex countryside, miles from anywhere, from anyone… except ghosts.

"I see what I want to see," I said.

"You construct your world."

And I had; I had retained Miss Tiggs in my version of reality, pretending that she still served me my meals when it was I that had been doing so, month upon month. What a thought to ponder on; what a notion indeed.

"But soon I will see things I *do not* want to see."

"That's when you need to draw on instinct, Rosamund, and act upon it."

"Be plucky?"

"That's right. You are equipped to deal with this. And there is more armour coming, I promise."

"Armour? As if I were a soldier, going into war?"

"There are always battles to be fought. This is just one of them."

Instead of questioning further, I yawned, and as I did, Josie and the room in front of me waivered, flickered from side to side, before becoming complete again.

"I believe I am waking up," I said.

"You are."

"Will I ever see you again?" The thought that I would not was untenable. Josie was but two or three years older than myself; no more than a girl just as I was a girl, and yet she was a mother too, or at least all I imagined a mother to be.

Perhaps sensing another swell of emotion within me, she stepped forward and put her hands upon my shoulders, fixing those tourmaline eyes upon me.

"Not in this lifetime," she replied and there was sorrow in her as well, so deep that I felt compelled to reach out and return at least a degree of comfort.

"We *will* meet again, Josie, perhaps not here, but somewhere." There was a pause before I added, "I know it to be true."

"How?" she asked.

"Because instinct tells me."

There it was! That radiant smile! Oh, how it captured me. How it enlivened me. It resurrected hope when hope had been buried for so long.

I yawned again. I awoke.

I *truly* awoke.

Josie was gone. All that I found myself clutching was the necklace, its stones twinkling.

I smiled to see it and then my smile faded.

There was another bang at the door – and this time it was real.

Chapter Sixteen

THERE was no escape, no one to help me, not now. I had to face him. Pit my wits against his. It was a battle and the only armour I had: a necklace that glittered.

As I secured it around my wrist, the cuff of my sleeve amply covering it, I thought of making safe harbour for myself also. The attic. Perhaps I could open the door, dodge beneath his arm, and run. He would not follow me there. *Why?*

"Rosamund!"

Father's voice almost deafened me as the door burst open. Upon sight of me, he stopped, and, for a moment, we simply stood there, as if he was bracing himself as much as I; as if there was a glimmer of fear in him too. Seeing this, my back straightened, an almost involuntary movement. Perhaps it was this that caused him to lunge across the room; to grab me by the arm; to haul me out of the bedroom and down the corridor – that spark of defiance.

Whatever had caught alight in me, however, rapidly dimmed as we continued past the corridor that led to the attic. I looked longingly at it; it was so close and yet so far.

At the top of the stairs, I dug in my heels. "Let me go." With my free hand I batted at him.

In return, he exchanged my wrist for my neck and slammed me against the wall.

"Do not issue commands at me, do you hear?"

Briefly, my eyes left his and I glanced behind him, to where there was a window. It was not yet full dark, but soon it would be, in another hour, maybe less. Out here in the countryside darkness arrived so completely. And within it, I would be trapped with a drunk and a murderer.

If I was really capable of constructing my world, as Josie had suggested, I would have done so now; I would have peopled it with a thousand Josies; a thousand Constances; I would have filled the house with them, wall to wall. And they would have come to my aid. But there was no Josie and no Constance. There was not a single soul that I could see. Not even the doughy outline of Miss Tiggs.

At last Father released his grip on my neck, the skin continuing to burn from his touch, and I began to splutter as my breath also found release. And then we were off again, downstairs, while I held onto the balustrade handrail with one hand lest I should trip.

As the kitchen had been Miss Tiggs' domain, the study had always been Father's lair. That was our destination and in it I knew I would be trapped further. As he shoved at the door, not with his hand, but with his foot, kicking it wide open, he pushed me through, throwing me finally into the chair, which squeaked loudly in protest. I looked about me, astounded at what I saw. There were pictures piled upon his desk, all of them drawn by myself. I had, of course, lost count of how many I had created over the years – with so little else to do at Mears House it must have numbered in the thousands. I thought many of them had been disposed of, but plenty had obviously been kept by Father, not just a few, but scores of them, dating back years.

"Father?"

"Look!" he ordered, pointing at them. His face was no longer ashen; it was bright red, from alcohol no doubt as well as from the efforts he had recently expended.

"These are my drawings." What else was I to say?

"Look!" he screamed again, grabbing at my chin and pulling me closer.

"I *am* looking!" I squealed.

Mears House was a perennial subject; the only subject I could think to draw sometimes, but there were a number of portraits too, of me, Miss Tiggs, the maid before Josie, a governess or two… and someone else.

"Who is this?" he said, pointing.

"I… I do not know."

He was not content with that reply. "Who is it?"

"I… I…"

I had sketched in the woman's hair, but because I had used a light hand, it was neither dark nor fair. The eyes were dark, though, and the face heart-shaped.

"I do not know," I repeated, although there were many likenesses of her.

"Rosamund," he barked, turning my face towards him so that I had no option but to stare into those narrow eyes of his. "That is your mother. How do you explain it?"

My mother? A nervous laugh escaped me. And then I remembered, I confessed.

"I have a photograph of Mother! I found it in the library, tucked between books."

He looked shocked, utterly shocked.

"She left something of herself behind?"

"Yes, yes she did. That explains the likeness."

He let go of my face and straightened, one hand

reaching up to scratch at the stubble on his jaw. "I thought I had rid this house of every single item relating to her."

Not her photograph, or her necklace, or me. Am I not also to do with her?

A shadow crossed his face and I tensed; my rebellious thoughts – *triumphant* thoughts – quickly concealed.

"Where is this photograph?"

I was loathe to tell him.

"Rosamund!"

"In the attic," I answered at last, a hint of rebellion remaining. He hated the attic; it was safe there.

His reaction, however, surprised me. He simply laughed and shook his head. "It matters not where it is, only *when* you found it."

"When?"

"Indeed. Tell me."

"It was… It must have been… three years ago."

"Three years ago? You are sure?"

Time was often a blur at Mears House, but that day had been a momentous day; unforgettable. "Yes, Father. I am certain."

There was no more laughter. He grabbed at one of the portraits, then another, and another, until he had a fistful of them, thrusting them into my face. "These are portraits of your mother; the same likeness; the same shading, and they were completed well before you reached thirteen years of age; when you were nine; when you were ten; when you were eleven and twelve. You had no idea of your mother's appearance back then; you could not possibly remember her, but still you were drawing her. It is proof I tell you, proof!"

"Father, not all of them are alike. See? There are

differences." It was true, there were, albeit slight. As for there being a likeness to my mother, yes, indeed there was, but that could merely be coincidence, my father also being guilty of seeing what *he* wanted to see.

"What was the colour of your mother's hair?"

I shook my head, bit hard upon my lip. How would I know? The photograph was black and white.

"I asked the colour of your mother's hair?"

"I... erm... red," I replied finally, having to pick a colour, any colour.

"That is correct, red! And her eye colour?"

I swallowed hard, knowing I had to answer. "Green."

"Yes!" He said, punching at the air.

"It is because of Josie," I said. "I picked those answers because of her."

"Josie? I have heard you mention her; calling out for her even on occasion. Who is she? Come on, tell me!"

"I... I do not know." A ghost or a spirit perhaps, but not someone frightening, for who could be afraid of Josie? She was goodness itself; a woman who – in the absence of a mother – had been the closest thing.

"Is this her?"

Having let the portraits fall to the desk, he now held several sketches of Mears House – the exterior views.

Again he grabbed me, the back of my neck this time, forcing me to look at what I had, by my own hand, sketched.

"I do not understand..." I began.

"Look at the windows and the figures depicted at them."

Figures? They were just windows, the eyes of the house.

"Is one of them Josie?"

One of them?

"Who are the others, Rosamund?"

Were there figures at the windows? It was shading, was it not? Mere shading?

I continued to stare at the sketches; I had no choice; remembering how, in the drawing room, Josie had stopped to stare at them too; how I had seen her at the window one day whilst out walking, and she had been waving… If it was indeed her. It might have been someone else.

It might well have been someone else.

Shading. Shadows. Figures.

There were so many of them, in every drawing and in every window, staring back at me. Clearly, these were drawn by my hand, but my eyes had refused to see, at least back then; but not now. *You have awoken remember?*

My father took a step backwards. Oh the look of him!

"You *can* see," he whispered.

Still biting my lip, I could feel the tang of blood.

"And if you can see, you can also summon."

Chapter Seventeen

I believed that I knew fear. I *did* know fear. But not like this. Never like this.

Summon? Summon what?

"Ghosts?" I whispered. Is that what he meant?

His voice was so derisory. "Rosamund, there is so much more to this than ghosts."

I began to rise from my chair, determined that I should flee this time. Outside, the night had taken hold; a cold night, a winter's night, frost in the air that would nip mercilessly at my toes and my fingers; but better that than the darkness that had now blossomed inside this house; that had consumed Father so completely. I could avoid the woods by heading down the gravel path, or... I could run to the attic.

"Sit!" he commanded, noticing how bold I was becoming.

I hesitated to obey, my mind attempting to calculate the lesser of two evils.

Evil.

It was not an exaggeration; every cell in my body acknowledged it. Evil was resident in Mears House this night and it wished to invite more in.

You are equipped to deal with this.

That is what Josie had told me. Should I continue to sit

there rather than take my chances and run? Should I trust her? Believe in her?

The decision was made for me. Father walked over to the door and, pulling a key from the pocket of his jacket, locked it.

"Father, what are you doing?" I said, aghast at this new development.

"Making sure," was his sole reply.

Sinking into the chair, I screwed my eyes shut as if by that very act I could shut him out too; as if that alone would protect me. My hands rested in my lap, clenched tight, my nails digging into my palms, deeper and deeper; the silence and the tension both thicker than any fog that London could conjure.

Having barred my exit, Father moved to his desk. There was a definite mocking aspect to his leisurely gait; he had no need to hurry: I was a fly entangled in his web.

All I was able to do was anticipate his every move, and hope that eventually he would see sense.

"Father," I urged, trying to hasten the latter. "You believe I can see extraordinary things, but you are mistaken. I cannot. I am an ordinary girl. I want nothing more than to live an ordinary life. Whatever you are planning, I want no part in it."

He did not so much as even glance my way as he bent to pick up the carpetbag he had clutched to himself all the way from London.

I tried again. "We could be happy here, you and I. We could perhaps freshen the house; make it brighter somehow; a better place to live in. We could employ a maidservant; a local girl perhaps; one that is looking for an escape from her own circumstances, because… because it is overcrowded. I do not expect she will demand a vast sum. There may be plenty of girls that would be thankful for such a position. In the past this was a fine house and we could make it so again. Please, Father, listen to me."

Rummaging in the bag, he paused. "We could freshen the house, could we? We could employ more servants? What with, Rosamund? What with?"

I shook my head. "What do you mean?"

"Money, you stupid girl! There is none available. It went a long time ago, on you and your dresses; on having to keep up appearances, it being essential for London; from a certain class so much is expected." His expression was nothing less than bitter. "No, no, no. Every last penny is gone. We are in debt up to our necks. But do not fret," he reached for the decanter on his desk, poured some whisky into a tumbler and downed it in a single quaff, before repeating the action, the alcohol as ever giving him ballast. "I have a plan. There is really no need to fret about any of it."

"What plan?" Again I was bold enough to ask.

"You shall learn soon enough," he said, finally retrieving what he was looking for and holding it up for both of us to see – a brown bottle, filled with liquid.

My heart sunk to see it. "Laudanum?" I asked.

Taking the time to down yet another shot of whisky, he eventually answered me. "You know it is not." He handled the phial more lovingly than I have ever seen him handle anything. "It is Scopolamine and early trials have proved very promising. This is a truth drug, because you, daughter of mine, lie not only to me but also to yourself. All those to whom it is administered find it impossible to deceive. When this resides in one's system, there is no imagination; there is no power to think or to reason. I shall ask the question and I shall receive the truth."

"You cannot force me to take it." There was a distinct quaver in my voice.

"But I can."

"I shall refuse to swallow it."

"Oh, you will swallow it, Rosamund, you will."

"I can see!" There! It was out, I had admitted to it. Would he leave me be now?

Yet another shot of whisky was poured. "Rosamund, there is something specific I wish you to see and when you do, I want no lies at that point; no denials. I need you to describe it exactly; to commune with it, via me."

"Commune?" The very word was enough to send shivers dancing along my spine. "I do not understand."

How calm he was; how sure of himself. "But you will, soon you will."

"Let me go please."

"Tell me, where would you go?"

I could not sit still any longer. Whilst his hand was halfway to his mouth, the tumbler refreshed yet again, I upped and ran to the door; pulling at it; banging on it; kicking it so hard I thought the bones in my toes might snap. It moved not an inch.

My father roared with laughter.

"If it's Constance you would run to, she is no more – she is dead. As for Josie, I do not think ghosts will offer much assistance. There is no one that cares about you; no one to come looking for you should you happen to disappear."

I swung around. "What happened to Constance, tell me!"

"It is of no matter now."

"Tell me! I demand to know."

How narrow his eyes were; like a fox, as cunning. "How many times must I remind you? You are in no position to demand anything!"

"Tell me," I continued. I felt I could not take another breath if I remained ignorant of the facts. The ghost of her – the apparition – the blood that had surrounded those once beautiful eyes – yet again it caused my own eyes to water. "Tell me and I will take your drug, willingly, with no force required. Please, Father."

"She was an addict," was his languid reply.

"Yes, yes, I now know that to be true."

"And predisposed to fancy."

"We all have an imagination, Father."

"We do. And hers was vivid."

I had to ask it. "Could she see?"

His laughter was so cruel. "Nonsense is what she saw; nothing but the result of an addled mind."

"And yet you would use a drug on me?"

"A different drug, remember?"

I nodded at his tumbler. "Different to yours as well?"

I was such a source of amusement to him that he continued to laugh.

"Did you kill her?" I whispered.

"Oh, Rosamund! Rosamund! I should have liked to; she was an impertinent madam, so certain of her charms, she thought she could blind anyone with them."

"She was beautiful," I declared.

"But spoilt. That fool, Arthur, guilty as charged."

I disagreed. "Constance was clever; she was determined, and she was to be an integral part of the changing world."

"Quite enamoured of her, were you not?"

"She was my friend, *truly* my friend. What did she see that caused her to gouge at her own eyes?" That is how Arthur had described her actions, and I knew it to be true.

"She believed she saw a ghost," again Father's voice was full of derision. "Oh, how excited the society became; she could do it, she could see beyond the veil! A ghost, a glorious ghost, smiling at her, with hands held out beseechingly. But then she panicked and started to babble. *I do not want to see these visions. I must shut them out.* She raised her hands and tore at her eyes so that she could not. Arthur bolted forward to stop her, but she pushed him aside. Before it could be prevented, she ran from the room, along the corridor, and pulled open the front door. Arthur shouted after her as did some of the others, including that fool Stephen, but still she would not stop. *This is wrong. It is all wrong.* Her voice was so shrill. I had followed Arthur the length of the corridor, curious as to why she had reneged; to discover what had now terrified her; but I had the good sense to hold him back at the door; to slam it shut before anyone could realise which house she had appeared from."

"How did she die?" I asked, my voice reduced to a whisper again as I envisaged Constance's bewilderment all too well.

"She ran straight into the path of an oncoming carriage." He paused. "It was a sorry end," he added but without sentiment; without any evidence of emotion at all.

"And you shut the door on her?"

"I did, to protect the society."

"A society you are still a member of?"

He shook his head. "Not after this night. Who knows whether in the future it may develop, but it is not for me. I have outgrown it. In truth, it was never for me."

Selecting another tumbler that stood next to the decanter, he began to pour the liquid from the brown phial, after which he returned his attention to me.

"You will keep to your part of the bargain? You will take it willingly?"

I would, what choice did I have?

He advanced towards me, holding out the glass.

"Sip it now," he said. "There is no urgency. We have all the time in the world. In fact, I rather think the world is ours for the taking."

As I sipped at the bitter liquid, which burned my throat, I had yet one more question.

"Why have you outgrown the society?"

He leant forward, his breath in my face; one hand reaching up to stroke my shoulder in a manner that made me grit my teeth. "Because, Rosamund darling…" how he dragged that last word out; how he injected it not with love and kindness but with a scathing disgust, "…I want more than ghosts. And I always have."

Chapter Eighteen

MY mouth was extraordinarily dry. Never before had I tasted whisky, but suddenly I was desperate for it; for any liquor that would reduce this wretched condition I was currently afflicted with. Aside from that, my vision blurred slightly, and I felt nauseous – as nauseous as the laudanum had made me feel.

Would this succeed? Would I speak only the truth whilst under the influence of this drug? Time would soon tell.

It was not just the Scopolamine in Father's carpetbag, it contained his notes as well, and these he studied patiently whilst I was sitting back in the chair, waiting for the drug to do its work. He held various papers in his hand, studying them, and at times tracing his fingers over the symbols etched upon them. All the while he was muttering to himself; the only sound to break the silence.

Or was it as silent as I believed it to be?

This was not a house given to groans and creaks. At times, when I lay awake in bed at night, I would wish for some kind of life, but it never came; just silence… and shadows. Yes, there were plenty of shadows, from as far back as I could recall, and they were silent things, too. Why was this? Because they wished to terrify me, even though I acknowledged them only in dreams, appearing as twisted, fearsome things, hence making me shun them further? Or was it because – like me – they were frightened also? They knew I would deny them. For years I was guilty of exactly that; at least my conscious self was, but not my sub-conscious, the latter guiding my hand. Only some shadows had stepped forward, Josie and Miss Tiggs; the others had all waited so patiently.

Until now.

From outside Father's study, in the corridor, there came a scraping sound, then a shuffling. Was it Josie who had returned to help me, or others, growing bolder at last; the past residents of the house of whom I so far knew nothing? There had been so many shadows in the townhouse too; in London itself. It seemed as if the whole world was filled with the dead as well as the living, clinging to whatever existence they could.

As Father gathered my drawings into a rough bundle and pushed them aside; as he placed his notes upon the table and remained bent over them, still studying them, and muttering, the nausea I felt threatened to overwhelm me.

"Father, I feel sick."

"Be quiet, Rosamund! Allow me to focus."

A moment later, he banged his fist upon the table.

"What is the matter?" I asked, my heart banging too.

"Some of this is hard to decipher." He said it more to himself than me.

"Is it Latin?"

He did not answer, but scraped his chair back, stalked over to one of the bookcases and selected a book. He thumbed through it, discarded it onto the floor and then selected another, doing this over and over again; the frown on his face growing deeper.

The noises from the corridor continued, but Father appeared oblivious to them.

"Damn it!" He said after a while, flinging the latest book from him to join the others in a pile at his feet. "I do not need books. I do not need Latin. I do not need *them*!"

"Who?" I asked. "The society?" Was it them he was referring to, his esteemed colleagues, pooling their resources in their relentless pursuit? Father had always appeared to me to be an educated man, but in truth I knew nothing of his education, not having talked of such things. Perhaps he was not as clever as we both believed.

Kicking aside whatever books lay in his path en route to where I sat, he grabbed the arms of my chair as he lowered his face to mine. "All I need is *you*."

I shrank back from him. He must have noticed, but he said nothing. He was consumed only with himself and his dark desires.

As he straightened, he reached for the chain of the ceiling gas lamp.

"What are you doing?" I asked, panic momentarily pushing aside any preoccupation with nausea.

"We need the darkness, so you can see."

"But I cannot see anything!"

"Do not lie. You must not lie."

"How can I lie when you have drugged me to prevent it? I am being truthful. I cannot see anything. Not in here. Please, Father, we need the light."

All too speedily it was extinguished.

There was a moment of quiet and then suddenly he began to speak, not in English, but in a foreign tongue. He knew something of Latin after all, it seemed.

"What are you saying? What are you doing?"

Receiving no answer I continued listening. The same words were being used continually, over and over. It was a chant, I realised, a summons. An icy dread prickled my skin and I shut my eyes to yet more darkness, my head spinning now as the drug increased its hold on me; the bile rising in my throat.

"I shall be sick, Father. I shall!"

He stopped reciting and hope flared within me.

"Father, I need a receptacle of sorts."

There was only silence – even those outside the door had fallen quiet as if they were as tense as I myself was; listening in, deciding whether to flee rather than witness what was being invited here. Father began again, his voice more urgent this time and punctuated only by the taking of more whisky. He always drank, and often to excess, but his drinking now appeared as frenzied as his words.

"Voco… deus magnus… abundantia… divitiae… Clauneck… Clauneck… Clauneck…"

Able to pick up on that last word in particular, I asked what it meant.

"Not what, *who*," Father answered.

"Then, who?"

"He is a demon; one who is capable of bestowing great wealth upon his loyal followers. I need to reveal him; I need him to understand that I will bend the knee; that I will serve him with the utmost respect; that I will do his will, in return for riches."

I listened with disbelief. "So it is true," I breathed. "You have become a mad man."

"This is not madness, this is truth! Tell me, is he listening? Does he show his face?"

"If he does, I will refuse to look upon him."

"You will refuse nothing, not if you know what is good for you."

The threat in his voice was all too obvious. He was my father, but he was also a mad man, a murderer and now a demon-worshipper. Was it possible he would murder me if I continued to antagonise him, again with his bare hands?

"Tell me what you see."

Just darkness. Utter darkness. Oh this nausea! I had to keep swallowing and taking a deep breath, followed quickly by another.

"What is the matter?" he said, seizing upon my breathing as some kind of gesture.

"As I have told you, I feel ill!"

"NO!" On his feet, his fist once again resounded against the table. "Stop lying to me. You can see something. I know it. The phial, where is the phial…"

"No," I echoed. "I shall not take any more." Also rising to my feet, I was amazed at how weak my legs were, barely able to support me. I had to feel for the desk in front of me and lean against it. "I have told you, I am going to be sick."

No sooner had the words left my mouth than it opened further and bile rushed forth, with such a violent eruption that it fouled the desk, the floor and myself. My stomach was aching as well as my head; convulsing as I stood there clutching at it. "Father," my voice was so weak, "what was that drug? I am so unwell."

When he spoke, my entire body flinched. He was beside me, although I had failed to hear his approach. For a moment I remained hopeful that he would not continue in his pursuits if I was sick; that he would allow me to crawl back to my bedroom to lay upon my bed and attempt to combat the toxicity of what had assaulted my system.

Yet again that hope was dashed as he grabbed my shoulders and swung me around to face his desk; standing at the back of me, one hand holding me against him, the other lifting my head so that I was forced to stare ahead.

"What do you see?"

"There is nothing here."

"Do not lie!"

"I swear, there is nothing, not even shadows."

"Call his name out."

"No... I—"

"Say his name!"

"Clauneck."

"Again!"

"Clauneck."

"Again! Again!"

"Clauneck. Clauneck. Clauneck."

"Does he hear you? Is he there?"

"No, Father. No."

"You need more."

He let his grip loosen as he continued searching for the phial. I turned my head in the direction of the door. If only he had not locked it, I would pick up my skirts, take flight and continue running, past whatever it was that shuffled and scraped – that resided here as well as me – all the way to the top floor, to the attic. And once there, I would push something up against the door, keeping him without and imprisoning myself within.

Father had found what he was searching for and, returning to my side, grabbed my head as he brought the drug upwards. I clamped my mouth shut as he jammed it repeatedly against my lips, the contents spilling onto my chin and drenching me further.

With one hand I managed to restrain him and turn my head enough to speak.

"Drugs open the doors of the mind," quickly I had to force the words out, "that is the opinion of one of your colleagues. I heard him say so."

To my amazement he halted in his endeavours.

"Father, if that is so, then *you* take it. See for yourself that I speak the truth. Demons do not exist. This... Clauneck does not exist. There is nothing there."

As he released me, I fell back against the chair. I could hear him drink – not from the whisky bottle this time but from the phial, desperation now forcing him to heed my words and act upon them.

There were tears in my eyes, from not only fear, or the reek of vomit, but – surprisingly – from sorrow too. That it should come to this between Father and daughter; that a relationship that was devoid of emotion could actually deteriorate further. And the medicine I had told him to drink. What if... What if...

I shook my head, the movement causing more waves of nausea.

I waited to see... As did the entire household, spirit or otherwise.

Father had taken his seat; was murmuring under his breath, those same words. *Voco... deus magnus... abundantia... divitiae... Clauneck ... Clauneck ... Clauneck.*

I peered as he peered, into the darkness. Still there was nothing, his chant taking on an almost whining quality – *Clauneck, Clauneck ...*

Father, how I wanted to say it again; *stop this. There is nothing.*

I was afraid of his reaction when he realised this to be true – that there was indeed nothing – as surely he must. Would the madness flee from him or would it drive itself deeper, thereby putting me at even greater risk?

As it sometimes did at Mears House, time became meaningless. I do not know how long we sat there; it may have been minutes; it may have been hours – and if it was hours, certainly the dark did not lessen; it remained as intense as ever.

Incredibly, I was growing sleepy. I found my eyes closing of their own accord and wondered if I should simply give in to it. It had been in dreams that I had seen Josie last; might she visit again, to offer the support I so desperately needed? But I had seen other things in dreams too – in nightmares. Did I dare to gamble?

Sleep is also a drug; one that was impossible to resist. My head fell forwards. There was darkness, but this time it was grey at the edges, and as soft as a blanket. *Josie? Josie? Where are you?* There was no reply, I called again. *Mother?*

A figure in the distance became apparent – a slight female figure, a curious light surrounding her.

Mother!

I was surprised to realise how easily hope could diminish dread. I began to run, forward this time, not back – and my feet felt light, as though I was not running at all; as if I was gliding, as Josie tended to glide. The closer I drew, the brighter the light became, but it was not painful, as staring at the sun would be painful; it was a light I wished to enfold me; to protect me; to keep me safe, forever.

Mother?

I drew closer, and yet still she remained out of reach.

How long until I could touch her? Until I could see her? Gaze upon a face I had only ever seen in a photograph?

You had red hair and green eyes. I never knew that about you, I never realised. It is such beautiful colouring, delicate even. Is it you?

That newfound hope refused to abate.

I want so much to see you!

Someone was calling my name!

Rosamund… Rosamund…

Love as well as light filled my heart – but instead of feeling as if it was going to burst, it simply expanded. I never imagined a heart could be so big!

I was smiling, widely, from ear to ear. I was old and yet I was young, just like Harry, I felt ageless, weightless, as though I belonged.

The figure was reaching out and I reached out too. Soon our fingertips would touch for the first time. No, not for the first time, surely. *How did you die, Mother? When did you die?* Not a word Father had said about her; not one word. Had she held me when I was a baby? Loved me? Comforted me?

The haze was lifting; she was becoming clearer.

This woman. Her hair red when mine was dark; her eyes green when mine were brown. This mother of mine, the necklace still in place, draped around her neck.

"Mother," I whispered, suffused with joy.

But that joy was short-lived.

How wretched she appeared close up; so many lines on her face and suffering etched into each and every one of them; such sadness and such despair.

No! It was not to be like this! My sense of joy must continue.

No! No! No!

How many times had I cried that recently? Too many, and yet it made no difference. No one heard my cries. Not now, not ever.

But I heard another cry well enough.

Chapter Nineteen

"FATHER, Father, what is the matter? Speak to me! What is it?"

I had woken abruptly and with one hand wiped at my mouth. It felt crusty, ingrained with filth. I looked from left to right, trying to understand what was happening – the reason behind such a commotion.

Father was no longer sitting; I could hear he was on the move and still crying, "No! No! No!"

With my dream pushed aside, if indeed it was a dream, I began to strain my eyes, desperate to pick out something; anything.

Still using the desk for support, I found my way around it, at the same time feeling for the candle that sat upon Father's desk, praying that the matches were close by.

"Rosamund," Father continued and his voice was a shriek. "He is here!"

"There is no one here." My intention was to remain calm and collected, although my hands were shaking hard enough as I continued to search. I found my way to the right side of his desk, for that was where I had last seen the candle. My hands reached out and sure enough, there it was; a small triumph, but one I was supremely grateful for. As if afraid it might disappear from my grasp, I kept one hand upon it, the other still scrabbling for the matches.

Were they on the desk too or in a drawer? If the latter, would there be time to locate them?

"He is here!" Father insisted. "I saw him. Hiding in the shadows."

The one searching hand becoming frantic now, I knocked over a tumbler and liquid splashed onto my hand, the peaty smell temporarily overriding all the others but hardly preferable. Where were the matches? We could not remain in the dark; we simply could not.

Here they were – a box that rattled when I picked it up. Another victory!

I had to work quickly; like Arthur before him Father was spinning out of control. Already I could hear banging and crashing as if he was trying to bat at something.

I was right. When the wick caught alight, it revealed Father close to the window, with his back to it and his head swinging vigorously from left to right.

If he registered the candlelight, he made no acknowledgement of it as if he had not noticed it at all; as if it was the one thing he could not see.

Although afraid, I forced my legs to move; the candle as much a shield as the necklace, which was still in my sleeve; safe. A few steps from him, I held the flickering candle aloft. His chin looked wet, as though it was covered in drool and his eyes were narrow no more, but wide and fit to pop.

I had been fixated on him, but I also needed to be alert to what else lay in the dark corners of the room; to see what had caused not just fear in my father, but terror.

There were shadows certainly, but empty shadows, I was certain of it; no one or nothing daring to encroach.

I reached out and tried to reassure him. "I can see,

Father. You know I can. And there is *nothing* hiding here."

Father slapped at my hands, as well as the air around him. "He is here! He is!"

Again I had to look, wondering if it was I at fault; if my wish had been granted and I was now normal and what ability I had, transferred to Father? An outlandish theory, but was not all of this outlandish? The shadows remained empty.

"Who can you see?" I asked at last.

"Him! Him!" he replied, pointing.

I looked at where he was directing me.

"I cannot—"

"Clauneck!"

Clauneck? "The demon?" I took a deep breath. My throat felt sore from my earlier retching and my head still pounded. "There are no demons. Demons do not exist."

Father tore his eyes from whatever had captured his attention, his lashes casting spidery shadows upon his cheeks. "You are wrong, Rosamund. There are; they do."

As if from a spring, he leapt from me and up to the bookcase. With both hands he began tearing at the tomes that lined the shelves.

"What are you doing?" I pleaded, desperate to understand.

"The answer," he gibbered, as around me so many hard-backed volumes crashed to the floor, their leather spines I imagined crumbling. "It will be in here somewhere."

There on the side table I spied the wax tapers, so took the opportunity to light one from the candle and set about illuminating the room with the ceiling gas lamp; a poor and dull light, but a welcome aid to the candle that I still held.

I drew nearer to Father; narrowly avoiding a book flung my way. "The answer to what?"

He paused, turned to me and once again I raised the candle. "He is not as I thought," he whispered as though now I was his greatest confidante. "He is…"

"Evil, Father?" I finished for him, as he seemed to struggle for words. "Did you think him a benefactor with no price to pay? Did you not expect this? You *wanted* to see him."

"If I served him—"

"Then you would serve the Devil, and no one and nothing is worth that."

"He wants my soul, Rosamund, but he offers me nothing in return. All his promises are false. He is a liar. Another liar, like you, like your mother." He lifted his hands to his hair and began to tug at it. "I am plagued by liars!"

I had to try and stop him. He was so agitated that it seemed he would tear it out if he continued, for tufts were already coming away in his hands. Placing the candle back onto the desk – feeling immediately bereft of it – I raised my hands too.

"Stop this! We can leave this house now if you wish; get away, far away; find safety somewhere. But I must reiterate, there is nothing here."

"LIAR! YOU ARE A LIAR!"

Tears sprang to my eyes that madness had him in its grip so completely. As much as I feared Father, I could not hate him – he was all I had, especially now – and without him I should be lost; another urchin on the street. And they were not safe, the streets; in so many ways they were not. I would be doomed; driven mad as well, surely?

Wiping at my eyes, sniffing loudly, I attempted to remonstrate with him again. This time he threw me from him just as he had thrown the books, sending me crashing against the desk, one of my hands flailing, trying to find purchase of some sort, to break my fall. In doing so, another of my fears was aroused. My hand knocked the candle, sending it flying to the other side of the desk where it teetered on the end and fell onto the floor, the flame not catching alight, trapping me in a burning room again, but snuffing itself out. As it did so, the ceiling gas lamp dimmed further and further, until it was barely even aglow.

"NO!"

Father's scream was spine tingling, as once more darkness reigned. I heard more banging and crashing as he hurled himself from wall to wall. In spite of my concern for him, I had need to protect myself whilst he was in such a dreadful state and so I crawled beneath the desk and curled myself into a tight ball.

Again time had no meaning; it may have been seconds, or it may have stretched into minutes that I hid there. Father would hurt himself severely if he continued; I dreaded to think of the bruises that even now must be blooming upon his skin.

I had not realised that I was crying until droplets of tears splashed upon my hands. Even if there was no demon, this was indeed hell, and I was in the pit of it.

If only I could close my eyes again; if only I could dream, but even in my dreams the respite was only temporary. Mother had not appeared to be at peace. Why?

Father was continuing to shriek; to scream, and instead of hugging my knees to my chest, I put my hands to my ears. Because I did this, it took me a short while to register that he had quietened.

"Father?"

I feared to leave the sanctuary of my hiding place, but as with the attic, how long could I stay there?

There is nothing out there, Rosamund, remember? It is all in Father's mind. The alcohol and the drug, when combined, were proving to be uncompromising.

That thought giving me reason, I began to creep forward, soothing him. "Father, I am here, be calm."

His shuddering form was but a few feet away. I had no desire to touch him but I forced myself. He was stricken, utterly stricken, but more than that, lost – reminding me of Constance; of Helena. Should one condemn such pitifulness, even if that person had brought it upon himself?

I touched his shoulder. He was in a position similar to that which I myself had previously adopted; curled into a ball and hugging his legs to him, like a child; as weak as a child, and certainly as vulnerable.

"Father, we must leave this room," I urged him. "It will be daylight soon, we can fetch help." Although from what quarters help would come, I had no clue; but surely there would be someone we could call upon. Never had I felt so alone. "All will be well, Father. It is the whisky, the drug. I believe that… together they have led you to hallucinate. But the effects cannot linger long; it will be over soon. All this will be over."

"No. No. No." His voice was childlike too.

"Father, let us take leave of this room; we can move to the drawing room, and wait there until morning. Then we can decide on a plan."

"Scared. So scared."

"There is nothing to be afraid of. All this… is in your

mind. Let me help you to your feet."

As I began to tug at him, I expected to be slapped or pushed again, but to my surprise he acquiesced. "That is it," I encouraged – able to act the parent, even though he never had. "We are on our feet now. Let us move towards the door. There is really no urgency, we can take one step at a time."

Having reached our destination, I turned to him.

"The key, Father, I need it."

"Yes, yes," he muttered, patting at his pockets. "Here it is; here."

I took it from him, my own hands trembling just as much as his, which at first hampered considerably the task of unlocking the door. Hearing the lock slide back into place, however, was a huge relief. I was about to open the door when I heard a sound coming not from the other side – a shuffling or a scraping – but from behind me.

Rosamund.

I turned to face Father.

"Why are you lingering?" he asked. "Open it!"

"Because you called my name. That is why."

"Me? No. No, I did not. Open the door!"

"But I heard you."

"It was not me." He was equally insistent.

"Then who—"

Rosamund!

There it was again, interrupting me – more assured this time, *amused* even.

"Yes," I answered. "Who are you?"

As something rushed towards me; something that hid no more; that propelled itself forth from the deepest part of the shadows, the umbra, the part where no light exists, and no light*ness*, I did not question further. I grabbed my father's hand, yanked open the door, and as I had done so often in that house; I ran.

Chapter Twenty

I had opened the door. Father had opened the door. Very different doors and for very different reasons, but nonetheless, both allowed access.

As we hurried the length of the corridor, I was most aware of two matters: there was something at our backs; but there were also other things; shades, more shadows. For this was not an empty house; it had never been an empty house; it was teeming with life... or more accurately, past life. And imagination, I was certain that this was at work too. *Imagine good things, Rosamund, only good things.*

Damn this corridor for being so long; this house for being so large – it was as if we could run forever and not reach sanctuary. The attic was where we needed to go.

I still had hold of Father's hand; pulling him; forcing him along – an arrogant, selfish, vain man – a man that had instilled such terror in me; who was so formidable. How easily he had broken. That was proving as much a revelation as to what my eyes could now see, the veil having dropped to the floor in many respects.

The attic – I reminded myself – we must get to it without delay. Whatever was pursuing us – and I had no wish to know what it was – I had caught only a fleeting glimpse, and that had been enough; more than enough – would not follow us into the attic. Of that I was certain.

Father will not go in there either.

Oh, he would! I would see to it.

At last we reached the hallway, a vast space with a tiled floor, which no moonlight dared to penetrate. The stairwell was to our left, a yawning chasm. Who knew what we should encounter upon it? I could not stop and contemplate. There was no time.

"Father, this way!"

I began to turn towards the staircase, but to my surprise I found myself jerked in the opposite direction.

"Father, no!"

He did not respond to me, perhaps he was incapable of speech, but even if that were so, he had certainly recovered enough strength to be the leader rather than the follower, and it was to the door that led out into the open air that he directed me. To the woods…

"No, Father! NO!"

I tried my hardest to redirect him, but to no avail.

We had reached the door and with one deft hand he managed to open it. Immediately we were hit by a blast of icy air as together we plunged into the grip of winter, both ill clothed for the night. Our feet skimmed over gravel then grass as we flew along.

My breath rattling in my throat, my eyes streaming with the cold, my body seized by it, I managed to look upward. Where was the moon? Oh, but to see a glimmer of it, shining down upon me. There was nothing; not even the stars.

The woods, that was exactly where we were heading, Father intent on it but mistaken in his reckoning. Those tendrils, those wisps; what if they came for me again? We would find ourselves surrounded on all sides; at their mercy.

What were they?

Did demons really exist? I found myself questioning my own beliefs. Did they not dwell solely within the pages of books? But what was a book if not a story? What was this life if not something of a story too? The boundaries between fantasy and reality, between *thought* and reality – could they blur, as the boundaries between life and death could blur? I had previously witnessed the latter; I knew it to be possible. On this night *anything* was possible.

We had reached the edge of the woods and, without further hesitation we plunged deep into them, the bare branches of the skeletal trees seemingly welcoming us.

I considered Father's study to be his lair, but this was a lair too. Once more I was trapped; my body, my mind, and my spirit. I began to tug at my father, my free hand attempting to liberate the one that was enclosed in his. Again, it was to no avail.

As we ran over decaying leaves, these once welcoming branches began to turn against us, as deep down I knew they would; whipping at my face and tearing at my hair. If they were doing the same to Father, he gave no sign, so determined he seemed.

"We must stop," I yelled, "or we shall fall."

It was as I spoke these words that Father stumbled; a tree root most likely the cause. His footing lost, he fell, and therefore so did I, nearly landing on top of him.

I had no idea if we had outrun what had previously been at our heels, but now was not the time to investigate – not in the woods, in the dead of night, the very air around us freezing our bones through to the marrow. I had never ventured to the other side of the woods, and to my young mind they went on forever; but there must be an end, and if we could reach it – reach civilisation; other people; *living* people…

On my knees, I reached out both hands, my intent to pull us up. To my surprise, I found myself tumbling further as Father's hands pushed me away.

I fell backwards this time, my ankle beneath me twisting furiously.

I screamed with pain as I rolled onto my side, clutching at the injured leg – not a broken bone, surely? I could still flex my toes. A sprain then? If so, all was not lost.

Rather than watch Father regain his feet, my eyes searched frantically for a stick, one that I could use as a crutch, almost willing one into existence. I believed I knew, even then, that Father was about to abandon me. And this time, it would be for good.

A stick. I had to find one. I had to get out of these woods; not to the far side, but back to Mears House, to the attic. Stay there until… Just stay there.

My hands encircling a gnarled length of wood, I dared to look up.

"Father," I cried. "Please, you cannot leave me."

He had resumed running.

"Father. No!"

Oh, the emotions that ran through my body and my very soul, in endless circles, smashing into one another, over and over – the anger, the bewilderment, the hatred, the terror, the betrayal, and as Josie had said, the grief. It was wrong to allow such emotions; far better to stay calm, but I could not. They engulfed me; we were as one – inseparable. But they were dangerous; so dangerous. The sheer force of them *attracted* things to me; negative things. They were doing so even now.

With no moon visible, the night was black, but those wisps that I had seen before, as slippery as eels, were blacker; and now they began to weave their way through the branches again, breaking off from the low cloud and becoming something else entirely. My jaw dropped open. I had a stick; I could haul myself up, but fear rather than the cold had rendered me immobile. Still they continued to weave, this way and that; seeking their quarry; taking their time; no need to hurry, just as Father had thought he had no need to hurry, I was not going anywhere. I could not.

There! With sightless eyes they had spied me.

Rather than wisps, they swarmed together to form a cloud of their own; a miasma; and as I watched, a part of me was mesmerised, fascinated even. Was it an ugly thing? Yes, yes it was that, but it was also beguiling. It appeared to want me and only me and that fact alone was seductive for none had wanted me before. What would it feel like to touch it? I let go of the stick and reached out. Would it be cold and hard, razor-edged? Would it shred my hands to ribbons, then my arms, and then my entire body? Or would it be something different; something quite unexpected? A void, but one in which there was at least a semblance of peace; a silence as profound as that to which I was accustomed; and I would exist at the heart of it, just as I had existed at the heart of Mears House - alone.

Tempting, it was so very tempting.

Indeed, after tonight, where else could I exist?

"Very well," I whispered.

I think I may have even smiled as the mass began to swirl; to concertina; dancing for me; toying with me, knowing that I had succumbed; that it was the master.

Not as ugly now, but really quite beautiful. In its own

way…

A scream – so wretched – pierced the trance I had fallen into.

Was it Father?

In the corner of my eye I yet again caught sight of something fleeting, and I tensed. Whatever *that* was, it was not beautiful. It was… obscene.

There was another shriek and even the mass in front of me shrank to hear it.

"Rosamund! Rosamund!"

He was screaming my name, just as he had done so many times before.

"Help me!"

My father. My jailor. The betrayer.

The spell broken, I retrieved the stick and struggled to my feet. The mass was no longer leisurely in its nature, but now had grown as frenzied as my father; angry perhaps at having had its carefully orchestrated performance interrupted. It was not beautiful and it had never been so. It was a liar. Another one. And I was not.

Not now.

My father's cries – his begging and his pleading – were terrible to hear. I had to reach him, convinced that whatever had him in its grip – *him*, I reminded myself, and not me; the thing that he had dared to summon – was now tearing him apart, growing teeth and claws that could rip into flesh and bone as if they were paper-thin.

But there was something that had me in its sights – still; that barred my way; that might not hesitate to do the same.

I could not help him. Why should I? He had never been generous to me. I could turn; flee again, as best I could. The attic – all I needed was to reach it.

I did turn, I began to hobble away, but that cry that filled the air; that 'please', drawn out with such terror… *But he is your father!*

Could I do it? Could I save him? And in doing so, would I save myself?

Harry came to mind and the message he had imparted about the necklace in Berkeley Square. *Protection.* Josie too, when I had stated – as if I had known – that soon I would see things I did not wish to see. Acknowledging this, she had counselled, '*That's when you need to draw on instinct, and act upon it.*'

Although my hand was shaking; although the night seemed darker than before; I reached into my sleeve and retrieved the necklace. I had to drop the stick to do so, for I needed both hands to drape it around my neck. It was armour, to be hidden no more. With the necklace finally in place, I turned back to face the mass, ignoring the pain in my ankle; my head that continued to ache, and the fear that wanted to cow me.

You can get tired of fear.

And I was tired. So very tired.

But I was also something else.

As my hand reached up to clutch at the stones about my neck, feeling their warmth penetrate my fingertips on such a cold, cold night, the energy that was at their core, *positive* energy, I realised exactly what – and who – I was.

I was Dickens, the creator of a character I admired; one that was plucky.

I was Josie, who had taught me the magnificence of the spirit world.

I was Constance, brave, tragic Constance; different, as I

was different; who embraced both the darkness and the light, as I must now embrace them myself.

I was Mother; a woman who had meant for me to know her, in some guise at least, and who was with me even now, offering what protection she could.

And I was Father, who had taught me perhaps the greatest lesson of all; to deny my fear; to push it back inside me; to contain it.

All valuable lessons when you could no longer run.

Taking a deep breath, I limped forwards.

Instinct told me that whatever lay before me, I was not to nourish it further. I might be connected to some in the non-material world, but to others there was no connection at all, and nor should there be; in spite of how much they might seek it.

I hobbled on, bearing down upon the leaves; listening to their brittle crunch as they disintegrated beneath me.

How dark it was; how loud the screams.

"No more," I said. "No more."

I was so close now. I could have reached out and touched the mass as just minutes before I had wanted to do. It hovered ahead of me but, I noticed, it seemed to do so with uncertainty.

How I smiled to see that. How it bolstered me further.

I continued walking, straight into it.

It was cold inside – colder than a December's night could ever strive to be; a cold to stop your heart; to suck the life from it. And it would. It surely would. Had it not been for the necklace, I would have fallen to the ground, a husk, to rot amongst things that already lay rotten there. But Mother's necklace was warm, and its warmth was as hungry for the cold as the cold had been for yet more cold;

as relentless.

In the heart of yet another hell, I saw what ugliness existed – every fear; every terror; every depravity and selfishness; every perversion; every murderous intent and all the anger and injustice which it encouraged; every petty, jealous thought that man had ever entertained, going around and around, endlessly, trying to make sense of itself; to become more substantial; to find something, *someone* to infect, to cling onto. I saw it and I continued walking, emerging the other side.

Knowing what I had just done, and that I had survived, caused all that I had carefully concealed within me to pour forth. I fell to my knees, the pain in my ankle no longer unfelt as great gulping sobs burst from my lungs.

I had done it; I had faced evil, the sum of all my fears, but was I the victor, truly? The things I had seen... what man was capable of... what could dwell so deep, if not within a person's soul then the cavities of his heart...

The darkness is a part of life; just as love is a part of life. You cannot escape it, but you can try and understand it, perhaps better than I.

To whom did that voice belong? Where did it come from?

"Constance?" I longed so desperately to see her. "Where are you?"

She was not anywhere and – miraculously – neither was the mass; it seemed also to have reached its conclusion.

All was quiet; there was no more screaming; no more cries; no one calling for me.

The darkest hour was over. Dawn broke to bring light back into my world once more.

Chapter Twenty-One

IT was not done yet. I still had Father to find, and he had run ahead of me. Why was he so quiet? What state would I find him in? And now, as imagination took over, as a series of visions once more flitted through my mind, he was a bloodied red thing; mere pulp, having been torn apart and ravaged; fed on as a creature feeds upon another in the wild, with nothing remaining to identify that he had ever been human.

Dread filled me. Again, I felt compelled to turn around, put as much distance between us as possible. How much could one person be expected to endure? But to turn my back would be to act as he did, and so I forced myself onwards.

What I saw shocked me even more than what I had imagined.

There was not a mark upon him. The only altered part of him was his hair. Always so dark, it was now white; pure white. I had read that this phenomenon could happen following deep shock but had not believed it to be true. He lay as still as the morning air, and the expression on his face – dare I say it? Dare I even hope it? – it appeared peaceable enough.

I had travelled to Hell and back and I had survived. But in spite of this fact, I was not invincible; I was not immune to all I had experienced that night. As I stood gazing down upon Father's face, his eyes closed forever, I could feel my body stiffening.

I was sixteen years old, soon to become seventeen. I fancied myself on the threshold of womanhood, but in that moment I felt very much the child, as lost as all those that had gone before me, my father especially. Had that which tormented him, the demon that he had called Clauneck, gone? Certainly, there was nothing here that caught my eye; no fleeting glimpse of a body, a creation of some sort, hiding behind a tree, ready to come rushing at me once again. But had I ever really seen him? Or had I merely reacted to Father? In conclusion, was that all this demon was: a creation. Something dredged up from the depths of a greedy man's mind – his mirror image, in other words? And if that was indeed the case, did that make him any the less dangerous? A demon was a demon, no matter where it originated. The wisps, however, I had seen them in their entirety. They had felt real – as real as Josie – attracted to all that was negative in me, whereas she... she was attracted to everything that was joy.

I could ponder it no more. I was spent.

Unsure of what to do with a dead man's body – for certainly I had not the strength required to drag him from his resting place – I embarked upon the journey back towards Mears House, alone. I came upon the edge of the woods soon enough, the mist not above the trees anymore, but covering the ground in thick layers.

For a moment I stood there, as I had done so many times before and looked towards the house with its many windows; its eyes. Yes, there were shadows at them, and there always had been – spirits I decided to call them, rather than ghosts, as it seemed more respectful, somehow – the shades of those who had long gone but who had also left something of themselves behind; their essence. I was not afraid. I had lived with them for years. Once human, they were *only* spirits. There were far worse things, I knew that now: born of the human mind, but never quite a part of it. Soulless, chaotic, desperate entities; as were all things born of negativity.

The mist soaked my boots and the hem of my dress as I drifted rather than limped through it, almost as if I too were a spirit. *One day perhaps, Rosamund, but not now.* When I died, would a part of me remain behind, forever attached to Mears House?

There was so much to think about; so much to discover. And I would face it, the unknown. I would make it my business to know it.

I reached the door to Mears House, still standing wide open, and continued to drift inside. There she was, Miss Tiggs, as sour-faced as ever. I stopped to address her. "You never did take to me, did you?" Her expression did not alter and so I shook my head. "I did not take to you either." There was only acceptance in my words.

As the townhouse had been, the entrance hall was crowded with people toing and froing: ladies, gentlemen, butlers, housekeepers and servants. It had never been this way in my lifetime, but it had been once, and this was proof. I could not make out these figures as tangibly as I could Miss Tiggs, but I could sense them well enough; how busy some were; how others tended to saunter; their happiness; their sadness.

Would I see Josie as I climbed the stairs? Would I see Mother?

On the landing, as I turned toward the corridor that led to another smaller corridor, I could hear the rattling of doors which drew something of a weak smile from me. All the times I had acknowledged the sound of it and attributed it to Josie, Miss Tiggs, Father or Father's friends, it had been none of them, but the others, all along. I fancied they were the closest I had ever known to having an extended family.

Behind me a door shut; a sudden sound that ordinarily would have caused me to jump or at least flinch. Now, however, it appeared normal, albeit *differently* normal.

There it was at last – the hidden staircase that led to the attic. I had caught Josie lingering at the bottom of it once.

I came to a halt in the exact place where she had once stood.

"Josie," I whispered. "Josie."

There was no reply.

If she had ever been there, she was now gone.

If, Rosamund?

Oh, why continue to doubt myself? There was no 'if'.

"You achieved what you set out to do," I said instead. "You equipped me." For the battle at least, the one I had recently fought. How many more battles would I face, however? Was I equipped well enough for them too?

I gently eased open the attic door and entered.

The little window at the back, to which I had often gravitated, allowed the light to penetrate; an extraordinary amount, considering its diminutive size. I had never once been in this room at night; surely there would be no light then; it would be as black as the rest of the house. I could not imagine it somehow. There would *always* be light here.

I needed to find a spot to sleep or risk collapsing where

I stood. Already my eyes were closing of their own accord.

At the rear of the attic, the shaft of light pleasant upon my face, I finally settled with my back to the wall; my knees once again hugged to my chest. The door rattled once or twice but I ignored it, succumbing to my body's desire to rest; simply rest.

I do not know how long I was oblivious to all around me, but I awoke to the sound of my name being called.

"Rosamund. Rosamund."

"Mother?" I said, blindly reaching out, but no, it could not be her, and not Josie either. This was a male voice.

I thought fear was done with me. Clearly it was not. It enlivened my senses and pulled me rudely back to consciousness.

"Rosamund?"

"Father?" I said, my eyes snapping open. In death was he more daring?

But it was not Father that crouched down before me; a realisation that brought only mild relief, for it was one of *them*; the society.

"Stephen?" I said, pushing my feet out in front of me, kicking with them, as I tried to escape him. What a maddened thing he looked with his blackened hair; there was black around his eyes too, the whites of them so stark in contrast. A demon. He was a demon. Another. The nightmare continuing... perhaps... perhaps it had only just begun. As I managed to push myself up onto my feet, my mouth fell open to scream as Father had screamed, *savagely*; but not a sound came forth. Instead, only darkness filled my mind, and as I fell, I fell into his arms.

* * *

"My God, Rosamund, what has happened to you? Am I too late? I'm sorry, so sorry. I should have entrusted my instinct; I should have endeavoured to get here sooner."

When I regained my faculties, it was to find myself on the attic floor, cradled in this man's arms. Initially, as I swam my way back to awareness, I felt a sense of relief, of peace even; but then I remembered who it was holding me – the young man, Stephen Davis, a member of the *Society of the Rose Cross*, the group I held responsible for Constance's death, and nearly my own. I began to struggle, my legs kicking out once more, my arms flailing.

"You... you... fiend," I spat. "Get away from me."

"Rosamund, I mean you no harm!"

Managing to put at least a small distance between us, I protested. "You do! All of you do. If you associate with mad men then you must be mad yourself."

"Mad?" he whispered. "Rosamund, where is your father?"

"He... He..." Although there were no windows punctuating the wall, I looked in the direction of the woods. "He is dead," I said finally.

"Dead?" If I could see the colour of Stephen's skin beneath the soot, I knew it would be ashen. "Did you...?"

"NO! It is not I that is the murderer here!"

Sobs began to wrack my body.

"Rosamund..." Stephen crept closer and dared to put his arms around me again. I wanted to kick and punch; I wanted to scream for him to let me go, but I simply had no fight left. Instead I let him hold me, surprised to find that, once again, there was comfort in the circle of his arms. He clung to me and I clung to him, and suddenly it was lighter at the back of the attic – or perhaps it was that I *felt* lighter. Perhaps the two are inextricable.

Eventually I pulled away and looked into his soot-rimmed eyes, noticing for the first time that his scorched hands were bandaged.

"You are safe," I whispered.

"So are you," he whispered back.

I remembered now how he had treated me. "You are not one of them?"

"Not now. Rosamund; there is merit in their aim, but not in their methods. There are some that take it too far; that do not know when to stop."

"Like Father."

"And like Arthur."

Fleetingly, defiance returned. "That man sacrificed his own daughter!"

Stephen shook his head. "She came of her own free will."

"But I did not! You tied me to the chair."

"I stood against that," he protested, reaching out and taking one of my hands in his. "Rosamund, hard as it is to believe, there *are* good men in the society, wanting only to understand the material world with which the spiritual appears to be so entwined. They are doctors, surgeons, and they are men of science. I myself am studying medicine. I work at a hospital in London and if you had seen as I have, patients near their hour of death; how they reach out to loved ones from long ago; how they insist they are present in the room; how joyous they become at this realisation, no matter their agony; how all earthly trials are simply…

forgotten, then… we cannot but wonder; try our hardest to make sense of it. That is all I was attempting to do. But men… even the best of men… and so easily the worst… can become…" again he hesitated, "…desperate. I am new to the society, but after Constance, after you, I am finished with it. I want only to live in this world; to help the living as I do. Perhaps it is *only* at the hour of death that we are meant to see."

Not always, I wanted to say, *not for some.*

"Why have you come to Mears House?"

"When I finally emerged from that burning room; when I ventured outside, I expected to find you there. I searched and I searched, but there was so much commotion. Finally I begged your London address from one of my colleagues and made my way there. At the door, I was told that you had left immediately for Mears House. I… I am ashamed that I turned back at that, thinking there was no more I could do and returned home." His eyes as he looked at me were so intense. "I roughly bandaged my hands – the burns are superficial, I assure you – and, exhausted, I fell on my bed and slept; but some hours later I awoke, and I knew… I just knew you were in danger. I had no time to clean myself up as I called for my driver to bring me here. It was unforgiveable that I had allowed myself to even sleep."

"How did you know where to come?"

"I have visited before, on just the one occasion."

Of course! He was the fair-haired man Josie and I had noticed when we had stood together in the drawing room and gazed from the window.

"Rosamund," his grip became tighter. "I am so sorry that I delayed."

"It matters not. You could not have prevented it. Not at the end."

"Prevented what?"

I shook my head as more tears began to fall. "I cannot explain now."

"Of course not. You have been through too much. Rosamund…" how gentle his voice was when he said my name, "…come back with me. To London, I mean."

London? Again?

"There is no need to concern yourself with me," I answered. "I am not alone here."

"What?" How perplexed he looked.

"I am not alone," I repeated, my voice barely above a whisper.

To my surprise, he released my hands and once again hugged me to him. Oh my sobbing, would it ever cease?

"Come with me, Rosamund, please. I will tend to you, I swear it. Our house is similar to the Lawton house; there are plenty of rooms in it. And Constance, what happened to her – how the society tried to shun responsibility for her death – I was against that too. I shall see to it that justice is done, and for her mother too of course; but those most responsible are already dead. Please, please come with me. I cannot leave you here. I cannot."

"I would be a burden to you."

"Far from it. It would be my family's honour to welcome you."

I pulled away and stared just as intently at him. "Why?"

He smiled, his teeth as white as his eyes, accentuated by the blackness of his face. "We can discover all the reasons why in the years to come."

A shiver ran through me when he said that, but it was

quite different to that which I had experienced before; it had an edge to it, but strangely no sharpness.

My instincts told me not to stay at Mears House; that this chapter in my life was over, but to go with him, to trust him – the man that had come racing after me, albeit with only the best of intentions.

I nodded and allowed him to lead me from the attic, along the corridor, down yet more stairs, past the hustle and bustle that only I could sense; the laughter – there was definitely laughter; a tinkling sound; a *bright* sound.

Miss Tiggs was at the entrance as we passed through, as we left the house of my childhood. I chanced a smile but it was not returned. Outside, Stephen's driver was waiting for us, huddled deep in his coat, the loud snores he was emitting disturbing an otherwise quiet morning. We listened for a few seconds and then we looked at each other and laughed, part of me marvelling I was still capable of doing so. Eventually, my laughter subsided as I remembered who lay cold in the woods.

"My father. What are we to do about him?"

Stephen thought for a moment, his brow also furrowing. "I will inform the authorities upon our return to London."

"They may hold me to account," I said, afraid again.

"No, they shall not. I will see to it. You are safe."

For the first time ever.

Stephen prodded the driver, who grumbled his way back into consciousness, clearing his throat in a rather pointed manner before taking up the reins.

Once seated, I looked back at Mears House from the carriage window. What would become of it?

As we drove away, I continued to look back; especially

at the attic, where there were no windows at the front. A thought struck me: Mother had left a photograph for me; she had left a necklace, both of which had been hidden. What if there was something else I had not yet discovered; something that *needed* to be discovered.

There is more armour coming, I promise.

"Rosamund." Stephen interrupted my thoughts. Having noticed me shivering, he was holding up a blanket, gesturing for me to drape it around my shoulders. I did so and he drew me to him, encouraging me to lay my head against his chest, the pair of us caked in filth and not minding one bit. *Safe. Right now, that is all that matters.*

And in that moment, happiness, *true* happiness, began to bloom.

Chapter Twenty-Two

'READER, I married him.'

I had a husband and I had six children – six! Five boys and the youngest – by several years – a girl: Sarah – a final blessing when we had already been blessed so much; a child who could see further than her brothers, which was something we encouraged; something we guided, Stephen and I. And, Reader, I also had a dog – a black Labrador, Jared, who sat with the children and adored them as we did – as faithful a companion as I had always hoped.

It was just before Christmas and all of us were in the drawing room of our townhouse in the Chelsea suburb of London – the Davis family in its entirety. Our eldest, Stephen, named for his father, was almost nineteen, and planning to study medicine, but oh, what a different life he had led compared to me; a comfortable life; privileged. Nonetheless I wished to think that he, along with all our offspring, was sensitive to others; not in the same way that I was sensitive, but in a way that mattered just as much; treating everyone as he would like himself to be treated – with respect and compassion. They all did; they made me very proud.

"Mama," it was my blonde-haired boy, Edward, speaking. "The tree looks magnificent!"

His brother Paul nudged him. "Look at the gifts

beneath it! Which is mine?"

"You will find out tomorrow," our youngest boy, Robert, assured him. "For tomorrow is Christmas Eve!"

Sarah had broken from the fray and gone over to the window. I knew what she was about and who would be there. He always came visiting at this time of year.

"Harry!" she said, her four-year-old chubby fingers pointing.

I went and stood by her side.

"I wish he would come inside," she continued.

I did too. I had beckoned him in on one occasion, but he had shaken his head. His place was outside, on the streets. He was an urchin; a guardian; a child with the eyes of someone who had lived a thousand years, or had been dead for the same amount of time. Guardians came in all shapes and forms; they could even be dogs or cats. Very often that was the case, something I had come to realise through my research at the psychical society; a society I had helped to found that was very different from the one my husband once belonged to; one he now shudders to remember; a society destroyed by its members' role in the death of Constance. Shunned by all in London, their endeavours came to nothing. In contrast our society was held in high regard. *I* was held in high regard. Our goal? Similar to theirs, it was to 'prove' as far as possible, to the sceptical; to those who were quick to damn; to those who clung to the constraints of a religion – a religion that strangely, believed in ghosts, provided they were 'holy' – that the paranormal existed; a world outside the normal – or what we, as humans, perceived normal to be. And this we did via a process of collation; collecting diligently the experiences of those who had encountered the paranormal; people willing to offer their experiences rather than be coerced into it. Of course I have included my own experiences, lately preferring to specialise in another area, one which a number of my colleagues chose not to study: that of the *non*-spirit, of which our understanding is still basic. My father's girl after all? No, for I seek to help them, not use them for my own personal gain.

Sarah was lifting her hand and waving.

"Yes, that is it," I encouraged, "wave to him. He enjoys that."

And it was not only she that lifted her hand, so did the boys. They saw what she was doing and ran over, accompanied by Jared, all of them, even my eldest, as excited by Harry's annual appearance as much as by the appearance of the Christmas tree itself.

"Harry! Harry! Hello!" Their shouting accompanied by Jared's barking amounted to a deafening roar, but Harry's smile became wider to hear it. The boys could not see him, only Sarah and I could, and, I think, Jared, for his eyes never strayed from the spot where Harry stood – but in our house such behaviour was blessedly common.

As Harry began to fade, I shooed the children away from the window, and gradually, one by one, including the dog, they left the room, involved in a game of *hide and go seek*. I resumed my seat by the fire and took up some paper and my pen.

Stephen bent to kiss the top of my head. "Rosamund, must you?"

"There are merely a few notes I wish to jot down and then I shall be done, I promise."

He took the chair opposite me. "You work too hard, you know that?"

"So do you," I countered, for he did, his work as a doctor consuming him sometimes, but he had stuck to the promise he had made at Mears House that day; he was finished with the dead, and tended only to the living. The dead were now *my* work.

Presently, I finished my notes and rose from my chair, crossing over to a bureau in which I kept my writing. The key was secreted in a vase high on a shelf. I retrieved it in order to open the bureau and place my notes in there. We did not hold with secrets, not in this house, but there were some things to which the young did not need access, at least not yet. Let them be children all the while they could!

When I had placed my notes neatly in one of the available drawers, my hand could not help but gravitate to another drawer, pulling at the handle to open it.

All the notes that Mother had written, at last I had found them – the final treasure.

"Darling, are you all right?"

"Yes," I said, my back still to him.

"Would you like some sherry?"

"Perhaps a small glass."

I heard him rise and cross over to the sideboard where the decanter resided. "Dash it," he cursed. "Empty. I shall ring for some more."

This time I swung around. "Why not save old Mrs Lovell's legs and go and fetch it yourself?" Rather like Miss Tiggs, she would be warming herself by the kitchen fire; *unlike* Miss Tiggs, she spoilt us, far too much, and I tried to reciprocate whenever possible.

"You are quite right, I will," Stephen conceded; dear Stephen, handsome Stephen; my saviour; my equal.

He left the room and as he did so, the lights in the

drawing room began to flicker. They often did, as if he took some of the light with him. A curious phenomenon and one I had documented, of course, in spite of the fact that he laughed whenever I told him about it. 'That is just you, Rosamund,' he would say, 'I doubt anyone else would notice a dimming of the lights when I left them.' I understood what he meant, but still...

Alone in the room, I withdrew Mother's notes. I knew them word for word, so had no real need to read them; I just wanted to hold them; to remember her.

We had gone back to the house years later, Stephen and I. I had an urge to see what had become of it since we had closed it up. I had had no more to do with it since, but suddenly, quite suddenly, something nagged at me to return; instinct I suppose you could call it.

The drive was as bumpy as I remembered; the villages, the towns, the countryside had barely changed, but the house *had* changed; it had fallen even more into disrepair – an old house, it had become as much a part of the countryside as the trees that shielded it.

As I alighted from the carriage; as I walked up the gravel path towards the front door; as Stephen heaved his body weight against it; as it finally yielded, I expected to sense at least *something*; the hustle and bustle of before perhaps. But there was nothing. The house was empty, quite empty; no furniture of worth remained and even the shadows seemed to have eschewed it.

"Where would you like to go?" Stephen had asked me.

"To the attic," I replied. "Just the attic, nowhere else."

His eyes were curious but he did not question further. He chose to trust me, you see, just as I had chosen to trust him all those years before. Implicitly.

In the attic, there was still that familiar shaft of light – my eyes watering somewhat to see it. This room, this sanctuary, why was it so? We began to search, the two of us, pulling covers from furniture, revealing not the twisted limbs I had dreamt of as a child but fine, sturdy pieces that had been allowed to remain, thieves not daring to venture in here either it seemed. We looked in drawers, in boxes and in old leather trunks.

"What are we looking for exactly?" Stephen had asked at one point.

"In truth, I have no idea."

"But we keep searching?"

"We do."

But oh, how frustrating it was proving to be, when time after time our search proved fruitless. My eyes were watering again when I eventually stopped to look around, not just dust the cause, but dismay.

"Perhaps I was wrong," I breathed, as much to myself as to Stephen.

"Darling," his hand was gentle as he laid it not upon my arm but my stomach. "The baby, perhaps we should…"

The baby – our first – was lying deep within me, just as something was lying deep within this room.

An idea formed.

"The floorboards. We need to check beneath the floorboards!"

"All of them?" Stephen had looked aghast at the idea.

"No," I said, trusting myself implicitly too. "I remember once stamping my feet, I thought there was a rat you see, in the corner, and beneath me a board rattled as if loose. Rather than unsettle it further, I moved away from it. Oh Stephen, if only I had unsettled it further! It was a sign I think, another sign."

"Where is this board?"

"There, where the light shines."

Where it had *always* shone; where I had sat when I was young; where I had slept and where I had cried. The exact light that had been in Mother's photograph; a light she had created – clean, as Josie had said – pure. That was where the notes were waiting for me.

Now I hugged them to me once more as tears erupted from my eyes.

My darling mother, how she had tried to help me; to let me know what I could not possibly have known as a child: that what I saw, what I sensed, what I had denied for so long because I was confused and frightened by it, was an inheritance from her. She described it not as a curse but a gift, but she warned me that there were some who would seek to exploit it, as my Father had sought to exploit it. There was darkness in mankind, she said, and because of the gift, I would be able to see it, and be vulnerable to it. And of that darkness were born other things darker still; that lingered in the dumping grounds, as I tended to call them, on the edge of our senses, but always waiting to break through; to be given a purpose; to feed and to multiply.

Oh, how I knew this to be true; how I fought every day to remain in the light. Mother, however, had succumbed, but not because she was weak. She was not.

When we had left the decay of Mears House, I knew I would never return; I would let the land have it; the trees creeping ever closer, their bare branches like the lover's hand I had once imagined – possessive. I had found what I needed – more armour in the form of validation; the truth, or *my* truth at least. It had attracted me to the attic but had repelled Father; someone who could not face up to what he was; whose own demons had destroyed him, a host of them, not just Clauneck. But more discoveries were yet to come. I could not forget the dream of Mother. When I had seen her in the distance, she had been a dazzling figure. When I drew closer, she had looked wretched.

She was a good woman. If she were dead, she would have been at peace.

If she were…

Like a woman possessed, I began my search for her, Stephen my ally as always. And we found her – we found my mother! Or rather a semblance of her.

She was in an asylum, in London itself, and had been since I was two years old. An old lady now: if her hair had once been red, it was now white; if her eyes had once been green, they were now as grey as her complexion. Stephen found us access to the hospital, one no better to my mind than the Bedlam Dickens had written about, a hospital that had long since been torn down. As I walked to her cell-like room I could hear the screams and cries of the inmates. They belonged not just to the living.

But Mother did not scream or cry, she was mute, quite mute, and although I introduced myself to her; although I tried to cling to her wrinkled hands and kissed her cheek a dozen times, she gave no response at all.

Locked-in Syndrome is what she suffered from, possibly caused by a stroke. A distressing diagnosis, it was not new to me as I had read about it previously in a book, fiction of course – Alexandre Dumas's *Count of Monte Cristo*, in which the character afflicted was depicted as 'a corpse with living eyes'. She was not expected to recover from her catatonic state and in that, the medical profession was correct, as she did not. She died four years later, on the eve that Sarah was born, and I liked to think at least something of her lived on in this child of mine, which was perhaps why I spoiled her so at times, trying to make up for what Mother endured.

As father had tried to bargain with the devil, Mother had bargained too, not with the dark but with the light, an even more formidable force. She could not prevent me from being born but she would make sure that the marriage produced no other issue, or rather pawns for Father to take advantage of. And me she tried to help in whichever way she could, through the photograph, the necklace, and her copious notes. *Remember me. I did exist. You are not alone. You are **never** alone.*

She had sent me Josie, I am certain of it; a woman so like her, who was there when I needed her most; who showed me what a mother's love could be; who taught me so well.

Anna Sarah Clermont was my mother's name and she had loved me; she had poured all her love into her words, until nothing was left inside and she had become a mere husk. Father had had no choice but to get her committed, because he was not a murderer, not then at least, that was to come as he deteriorated further; as he succumbed. The asylum, as grim as it was, had also provided her with sanctuary. There may have been indignities visited upon her, but the wall of light she had built would have offered further sanctuary still. Often I consoled myself with that thought.

Alone still in the drawing room, as Stephen had not yet

returned, I wandered back to the window and looked out.

There are things one should never see. And there are things one should never be: intolerant, selfish, vain and greedy, but at times, we are; it is human nature, only natural. For as long as we maintain some semblance of balance, we can walk the line well enough. When we fall, however, the danger is that we fall into the abyss.

Harry is no longer out there; he has now gone; but there are others. Sarah cannot see them yet; she can only see what is good. But Father opened my eyes a long time ago to what else exists.

Waiting for my glass of sherry, I clutched at my necklace, feeling the warmth of the stones flood through me, and their staunch protection. I could feel Josie too, and Mother, as well as the lingering presence of my husband, my children and my dog, though they were in other parts of the house. I could feel Constance, and I marvelled at how happy she was, caught up in the throes of yet another journey. We were, as Josie had said, connected. Together, we stood against what waited in the shadows, although I lifted a hand, and I acknowledged it. I had only pity for it, you see; this thing that knows not where it belongs, only that it cries out; that it is hungry; that it is insatiable. It cannot harm me, however; not when such light surrounds me.

And that is the thing; the light is there if you look for it. It is there in abundance.

This is a good time to be alive.

Constance said that to me, and I agree, wholeheartedly. I have walked through Hell and I have emerged, to find that life is *surprisingly* good.

And that is why *I* write, not to alarm or to instill dread

or fear into others, but to dispel ignorance, for ignorance is our greatest foe. If we remain in it, we remain lost.

The door opened and Stephen entered, brandishing the sherry.

"Sorry I took so long, darling, the damned bottle was hiding at the back of the cupboard. We had the devil's own job trying to find it, Mrs Lovell and I."

I laughed at his words, which were delivered with such innocence.

The devil's own job.

I write to keep the light shining.

The End

Also by the author

Eve: A Christmas Ghost Story
(Psychic Surveys Prequel)

What do you do when a whole town is haunted?

In 1899, in the North Yorkshire market town of Thorpe Morton, a tragedy occurred; 59 people died at the market hall whilst celebrating Christmas Eve, many of them children. One hundred years on and the spirits of the deceased are restless still, 'haunting' the community, refusing to let them forget.

In 1999, psychic investigators Theo Lawson and Ness Patterson are called in to help, sensing immediately on arrival how weighed down the town is. Quickly they discover there's no safe haven. The past taints everything.

Hurtling towards the anniversary as well as a new millennium, their aim is to move the spirits on, to cleanse the atmosphere so everyone – the living and the dead – can start again. But the spirits prove resistant and soon Theo and Ness are caught up in battle, fighting against something that knows their deepest fears and can twist them in the most dangerous of ways.

They'll need all their courage to succeed and the help of a little girl too – a spirit who didn't die at the hall, who shouldn't even be there…

Psychic Surveys Book One:
The Haunting Of Highdown Hall

"Good morning, Psychic Surveys. How can I help?"

The latest in a long line of psychically-gifted females, Ruby Davis can see through the veil that separates this world and the next, helping grounded souls to move towards the light - or 'home' as Ruby calls it. Not just a job for Ruby, it's a crusade and one she wants to bring to the High Street. Psychic Surveys is born.

Based in Lewes, East Sussex, Ruby and her team of freelance psychics have been kept busy of late. Specialising in domestic cases, their solid reputation is spreading - it's not just the dead that can rest in peace but the living too. All is threatened when Ruby receives a call from the irate new owner of Highdown Hall. Film star Cynthia Hart is still in residence, despite having died in 1958.

Winter deepens and so does the mystery surrounding Cynthia. She insists the devil is blocking her path to the light long after Psychic Surveys have 'disproved' it. Investigating her apparently unblemished background, Ruby is pulled further and further into Cynthia's world and the darkness that now inhabits it. For the first time in her career, Ruby's deepest beliefs are challenged.

Does evil truly exist?

And if so, is it the most relentless force of all?

Psychic Surveys Book Two: Rise to Me

"This isn't a ghost we're dealing with. If only it were that simple…"

Eighteen years ago, when psychic Ruby Davis was a child, her mother – also a psychic – suffered a nervous breakdown. Ruby was never told why. "It won't help you to know," the only answer ever given. Fast forward to the present and Ruby is earning a living from her gift, running a high street consultancy – Psychic Surveys – specialising in domestic spiritual clearance.

Boasting a strong track record, business is booming. Dealing with spirits has become routine but there is more to the paranormal than even Ruby can imagine. Someone – something – stalks her, terrifying but also strangely familiar. Hiding in the shadows, it is fast becoming bolder and the only way to fight it is for the past to be revealed – no matter what the danger.

When you can see the light, you can see the darkness too.

And sometimes the darkness can see you.

Psychic Surveys Book Three: 44 Gilmore Street

"We all have to face our demons at some point."

Psychic Surveys – specialists in domestic spiritual clearance – have never been busier. Although exhausted, Ruby is pleased. Her track record as well as her down-to-earth, no-nonsense approach inspires faith in the haunted, who willingly call on her high street consultancy when the supernatural takes hold.

But that's all about to change.

Two cases prove trying: 44 Gilmore Street, home to a particularly violent spirit, and the reincarnation case of Elisha Grey. When Gilmore Street attracts press attention, matters quickly deteriorate. Dubbed the 'New Enfield', the 'Ghost of Gilmore Street' inflames public imagination, but as Ruby and the team fail repeatedly to evict the entity, faith in them wavers.

Dealing with negative press, the strangeness surrounding Elisha, and a spirit that's becoming increasingly territorial, Ruby's at breaking point. So much is pushing her towards the abyss, not least her own past. It seems some demons just won't let go…

Psychic Surveys Book Four: Old Cross Cottage

It's not wise to linger at the crossroads…

In a quiet Dorset Village, Old Cross Cottage has stood for centuries, overlooking the place where four roads meet. Marred by tragedy, it's had a series of residents, none of whom have stayed for long. Pink and pretty, with a thatched roof, it should be an ideal retreat, but as new owners Rachel and Mark Bell discover, it's anything but.

Ruby Davis hasn't quite told her partner the truth. She's promised Cash a holiday in the country but she's also promised the Bells that she'll investigate the unrest that haunts this ancient dwelling. Hoping to combine work and pleasure, she soon realises this is a far more complex case than she had ever imagined.

As events take a sinister turn, lives are in jeopardy. If the terrible secrets of Old Cross Cottage are ever to be unearthed, an entire village must dig up its past.

Psychic Surveys Book Five: Descension

"This is what we're dealing with here, the institutionalised…"

Brookbridge housing estate has long been a source of work for Psychic Surveys. Formerly the site of a notorious mental hospital, Ruby and her team have had to deal with spirits manifesting in people's homes, still trapped in the cold grey walls of the asylum they once inhabited. There've been plenty of traumatic cases but never a mass case - until now.

The last remaining hospital block is due to be pulled down, a building teeming with spirits of the most resistant kind, the institutionalised. With the help of a newfound friend, as well as Cash and her colleagues, Ruby attempts to tackle this mammoth task. At the same time her private life is demanding attention, unravelling in ways she could never imagine.

About to delve deep into madness, will she ever find her way back?

Blakemort:
A Psychic Surveys Companion Novel
(Book One)

"That house, that damned house. Will it ever stop haunting me?"

After her parents' divorce, five-year old Corinna Greer moves into Blakemort with her mother and brother. Set on the edge of the village of Whitesmith, the only thing attractive about it is the rent. A 'sensitive', Corinna is aware from the start that something is wrong with the house. Very wrong.

Christmas is coming but at Blakemort that's not something to get excited about. A house that sits and broods, that calculates and considers, it's then that it lashes out - the attacks endured over five years becoming worse. There are also the spirits, some willing residents, others not. Amongst them a boy, a beautiful, spiteful boy...

Who are they? What do they want? And is Corinna right when she suspects it's not just the dead the house traps but the living too?

Thirteen:
A Psychic Surveys Companion Novel
(Book Two)

Don't leave me alone in the dark…

In **1977**, Minch Point Lighthouse on Skye's most westerly tip was suddenly abandoned by the keeper and his family – no reason ever found. In the decade that followed, it became a haunt for teenagers on the hunt for thrills. Playing Thirteen Ghost Stories, they'd light thirteen candles, blowing one out after every story told until only the darkness remained.

In **1987**, following her success working on a case with Sussex Police, twenty-five year old psychic, Ness Patterson, is asked to investigate recent happenings at the lighthouse. Local teen, Ally Dunn, has suffered a breakdown following time spent there and is refusing to speak to anyone. Arriving at her destination on a stormy night, Ness gets a terrifying insight into what the girl experienced.

The case growing ever more sinister, Ness realises: some games should never be played.

This Haunted World Book One: The Venetian

Welcome to the asylum…

2015

Their troubled past behind them, married couple, Rob and Louise, visit Venice for the first time together, looking forward to a relaxing weekend. Not just a romantic destination, it's also the 'most haunted city in the world' and soon, Louise finds herself the focus of an entity she can't quite get to grips with – a 'veiled lady' who stalks her.

1938

After marrying young Venetian doctor, Enrico Sanuto, Charlotte moves from England to Venice, full of hope for the future. Home though is not in the city; it's on Poveglia, in the Venetian lagoon, where she is set to work in an asylum, tending to those that society shuns. As the true horror of her surroundings reveals itself, hope turns to dust.

From the labyrinthine alleys of Venice to the twisting, turning corridors of Poveglia, their fates intertwine. Vengeance only waits for so long…

This Haunted World Book Two: The Eleventh Floor

A snowstorm, a highway, a lonely hotel…

Devastated by the deaths of her parents and disillusioned with life, Caroline Daynes is in America trying to connect with their memory. Travelling to her mother's hometown of Williamsfield in Pennsylvania, she is caught in a snowstorm and forced to stop at The Egress hotel – somewhere she'd planned to visit as her parents honeymooned there.

From the moment she sets foot inside the lobby and meets the surly receptionist, she realises this is a hotel like no other. Charming and unique, it seems lost in time with a whole cast of compelling characters sheltering behind closed doors.

As the storm deepens, so does the mystery of The Egress. Who are these people she's stranded with and what secrets do they hide? In a situation that's becoming increasingly nightmarish, is it possible to find solace?

Jessa*mine*
The Jessamine series Book One

"The dead of night, Jess, I wish they'd leave me alone."

Jessamin Wade's husband is dead - a death she feels wholly responsible for. As a way of coping with her grief, she keeps him 'alive' in her imagination - talking to him every day, laughing with him, remembering the good times they had together. She thinks she will 'hear' him better if she goes somewhere quieter, away from the hustle and bustle of her hometown, Brighton. Her destination is Glenelk in the Highlands of Scotland, a region her grandfather hailed from and the subject of a much-loved painting from her childhood.

Arriving in the village late at night, it is a bleak and forbidding place. However, the house she is renting - Skye Croft - is warm and welcoming. Quickly she meets the locals. Her landlord, Fionnlagh Maccaillin, is an ex-army man with obvious and not so obvious injuries. Maggie, who runs the village shop, is also an enigma, startling her with her strange 'insights'. But it is Stan she instantly connects with. Maccaillin's grandfather and a frail, old man, he is grief-stricken from the recent loss of his beloved Beth.

All four are caught in the past. All four are unable to let go. Their lives entwining in mysterious ways, can they help each other to move on or will they always belong to the ghosts that haunt them?

Comraich
The Jessamine Series Book Two

"The dead of night, Jess, I wish they'd leave me alone."

Comraich – Gaelic for *Sanctuary* – that's what this ancient fortress of a house in the Highlands of Scotland has offered its generations, a haven from the world beyond.

The nesting instinct kicking in, a pregnant Jessamin decides that Comraich, which she shares with her partner Fionnlagh Maccaillin, needs refreshing. Getting to work in one of the spare bedrooms she makes a startling discovery, one that pulls her into a world of the intense and disturbing passions of others that have been here before.

Jessamin has to decide.

Will delving deeper into Comraich's history bring hope and peace to this troubled house or return her to a darkness she's only recently left behind?

www.shanistruthers.com

Printed in Great Britain
by Amazon